For one night, instinct ruled her

When Scott came out of the bathroom, Gwen was waiting for him in the bedroom. If he was surprised, or even shocked, he dismissed it with a grin. "What can I do for you, pretty lady?"

Gwen heard herself respond. "Kiss me."

Scott let the shirt and suit he had half lifted fall back onto the bed. He straightened and turned, his eyes slowly sweeping her and examining her, welcoming her, yet questioning. "We might not make our reservation," he said softly.

At first Gwen did not know why she had come here—to talk to him, she supposed, to be with him for a minute while these new and confusing emotions and ideas were fighting their way for acceptance within her. Now she knew exactly why she had come.

"I don't care," she answered and stepped into his arms.

Books by Rebecca Flanders

These books may be available at your local bookseller.

Don't miss any of our special offers. Write to us at the following address for information on our newest releases.

Harlequin Reader Service
P.O. Box 52040, Phoenix, AZ 85072-2040
Canadian address: P.O. Box 2800, Postal Station A,
5170 Yonge St., Willowdale, Ont. M2N 6J3

Uncertain Images
REBECCA FLANDERS

Harlequin Books

TORONTO • NEW YORK • LONDON
AMSTERDAM • PARIS • SYDNEY • HAMBURG
STOCKHOLM • ATHENS • TOKYO • MILAN

Published September 1985

First printing July 1985

ISBN 0-373-16118-2

Printed In Canada

Chapter One

"Scott Stewart?" Annalee's eyes widened behind wire-rimmed glasses as she turned from the typewriter to stare at her friend. "The house on Beachwood Lane?"

Gwendolyn Blackshire grunted an absent affirmative and struggled with the tiny pearl button at the back of her high-necked blouse. The soft crepe material was slippery and the buttonhole refused to cooperate. "Get this, will you, Annie?" She lowered herself as far as the tight tweed skirt would allow to accommodate Annalee's position at the desk, pushing her hair away from her neck. "Why do they make buttons so big and buttonholes so small?"

But Annalee only stared at her. "Do you have any idea who he *is*?" she demanded breathlessly.

"Here, let me." Tim came up behind her and took the material between his fingers. He moved his face around to hers with an exaggerated leer and added, "You did say you wanted it off, didn't you?"

"Hurry up, Tim," Gwen complained. "I want to get out of here."

"Be still, my heart," said Tim, sighing. "If only you knew how often I've dreamed..." But he fastened the button, and Gwen swung away from him with a flashing smile and a pat on his cheek. Hurriedly, she gathered up her purse and her jacket from Annalee's desk.

It had been a quiet day for the Paos County sheriff's department, as much as any day could be considered quiet around the place Gwen affectionately referred to as "The Squirrel Cage." Six hundred square miles of mostly rural territory kept Gwen and the four other deputies woefully overworked, and it was rare that she ever left the office on time. She was terrified that the phone might ring with some long-overdue emergency before she made her escape, and her conscience would not let her desert Sheriff Brannigan when he was already two men short on the evening shift.

"You *don't* know, do you?" insisted Annie incredulously.

"All I know is I've got to serve a subpoena out on Beachwood Lane," Gwen replied, quickly running a comb through her thick dark hair, "and I'd like to get it done before midnight. People tend to get a little cranky when you get them out of bed for such things." She winked at Annalee and dropped the comb into her purse.

"You're going all the way out to the beach tonight?" Tim interrupted, frowning a little.

Gwen smiled indulgently and touched his arm as she inched past. "I *live* all the way out at the beach, remember?"

Tim was still frowning, assuming his overprotective fatherly act that Gwen found both adorable and exasperating. "How come you always pick up the subpoena assignments?" he demanded. "You act like you want to do them. You don't even know how dangerous it is—"

Gwen's eyebrows shot up in mock indignation at the familiar argument. "And the rest of the stuff that goes on around here isn't?"

"You know perfectly well what I mean."

"Scott Stewart!" Annalee practically squealed. "*Rick Stewart's* little brother!"

Both Tim and Gwendolyn looked at her. Tim in annoyance, Gwen in surprise. As a matter of fact, she had not made the connection. She accepted her assignments as given and rarely thought about the person behind the name and address on the cover of the legal paper. If she thought about them, she would inevitably begin to feel sorry for them, and she could hardly do her job if the softer side of her nature were allowed to intrude.

But this was different. Rick Stewart. "Well, I'll be damned," she murmured softly, her eyes reflecting appreciation for Annalee's astuteness. "I guess it is the same person."

Annalee nodded eagerly, and Tim interjected, puzzled, "Rick Stewart's place is near you? I thought he lived in Los Angeles."

"He doesn't live anywhere anymore," Gwen reminded him gently. Even though she herself had never been one of Stewart's more ardent worshipers, it was hard to refer to the legend without a note of reverence in one's voice. "His house—shrine, mausoleum, or whatever—is in L.A., but his brother has a house on the beach around here.... Don't you remember reading about it in the papers last year?" Of course, saying that Beachwood Lane was near Gwen's own modest cottage was like saying that Harlem was near Central Park West—a lot more separated the two places than miles. But she had never realized before that she had a celebrity living just down the street.

"Wendy," Annalee began impatiently, and at Gwen's frown, quickly corrected, "Gwen, tell us. What's he being sued for?" she demanded breathlessly.

Gwen's scowl deepened, but there was more playful exasperation in her expression than annoyance. "You know I couldn't tell you that, even if I knew." And she shrugged. "Probably nothing. Guys like that probably get eight or ten of these a day."

She walked a few steps to the partition that separated the reception area from the officers' desks and called out, "I'm out of here, guys! See you in the morning!"

The three men—two from the day shift and one from the evening—looked up from drinking their coffee and shooting the breeze, and grinned and waved, some giving a few friendly wolf whistles. Their attitude toward Gwen always made her feel warm inside. Acceptance had not been so easy when she first joined the sheriff's department a little over two years ago. Their respect was all the more precious because it had been hard-earned.

Tim, neglecting his stern paternal role, as he always did when he realized it made no impression, merely called out automatically, "Be careful," and Gwen turned to him with a wink.

"Don't worry, pardner," she drawled. "I can shoot the eyeballs out of a rattlesnake at forty paces."

Tim grinned and Annalee protested, "You could at least tell us—"

Gwen closed the door behind her.

The sun was setting over the Pacific, and the chill of the evening came quickly this far north. Gwen slipped her arms into the jacket of her tweed suit and shivered a little, digging her car keys from her pocket. She knew she was over-dressed for her task, but assignments like this went a lot more easily when the parties in question were not alerted in advance by a sheriff's department uniform. Besides, after being confined in khaki all day, Gwen liked to feel pretty and feminine whenever she could. She would never be able to run or jump in the slim-fitting, calf-length skirt she was wearing now—not without popping eight of the ten buttons that closed it down the side—and the soft draping lines of the white blouse were hardly apt for target practice. But she liked the way the silky material felt against her skin, and the high neckline made her dark eyes seem almost black and twice as large in contrast with the whiteness of the blouse.

Jeans and a sweat shirt would probably have been more appropriate for the type of gathering she was about to attend, Gwen reflected as she backed her dusty-yellow hatchback out of the parking lot. That, or leather hip boots and a sequined miniskirt. She did not know what kind of parties Scott Stewart gave, but she was willing to bet none of the guests would be dressed in suits.

Gwen had been in this business long enough to become proficient at it, and she saved herself a lot of legwork by researching a few particulars in advance. A simple phone call to Scott Stewart's answering service, claiming to be a girl friend who had forgotten the address of the place where Scott was planning to meet her that night, provided her with all the information she needed about the most efficient way to corner Scott Stewart. He was giving a party tonight at his own house, and it couldn't be more perfect—ease of access, plenty of witnesses. Gwen congratulated herself with a chuckle and turned up the volume of the car radio, singing along as she headed toward the coastal highway.

It wasn't always so simple, of course, but Tim was exaggerating about the danger. Process serving was the easiest part of her job, and Gwen had gotten used to outthinking the devious mind and shrugging off personal affronts. Only last week she had chased a bankrupt businessman through five bars, a Chinese restaurant and a car wash before finally cornering him in—of all places—his lawyer's office. Once a distraught man being sued for divorce had pointed a water pistol at her chest. She had received streams of abuse and heated threats upon her life, and had dodged flying missiles as she made quick exits, but all of that was part of the job. And this one was going to be a piece of cake.

It was a forty-five-minute drive from the coun-

ty seat to the beach, and although Gwen sometimes—especially at six-thirty in the morning—
hated it, she knew she would never choose to live
anywhere else. The beach cottage had been her
father's retirement home. He had worked all his
life toward the goal of retiring at the beach, with
his fishing poles and metal detector; he had been
in the little cottage less than two weeks before he
was dead of an arterial aneurysm. That had been
five years ago, and even if Gwen had not loved
the beach for its own sake, she would never have
been able to part with the ramshackle little place
that symbolized all the hopes and dreams her
father had not lived to enjoy.

It was an expense, commuting back and forth
everyday, and an inconvenience. Sometimes,
when she couldn't break away at even a reasonably decent hour, she spent the night in town with
Annalee or Tim, both childhood friends who simply couldn't understand why she would prefer the
isolation of the beach to a cheaper, more centrally
located apartment. They forgot their objections,
however, during the summer, when they—along
with all of Gwen's numerous other friends, their
spouses, children and in-laws—spent more time
at her place than they did at their own.

It was just after seven and fully dark when
Gwen pulled off the highway and into the last taco
stand before the sparsity of civilization gave way
completely to windswept dunes. She was officially
still on duty, and she probably should have dis-
patched her errand and gotten it out of the way
before attending to her own needs, but matters
were not run that rigorously in the Paos County

sheriff's department. Scott Stewart was not going
anywhere, and Gwen was hungry.

She placed her order at the takeout window and
thought absently about Scott Stewart as the car sat
idling. Gwendolyn Blackshire was not a person
easily impressed, but she could not help marveling a little over the twist of fate that would bring
her into contact, even secondhand, with so powerful a legend, and over the fact that she had
never before even realized that she was practically
living next door to a celebrity.

Not that Scott Stewart himself rated that status—until his brother's death last year and the
subsequent article in the paper when Scott had
moved into the beach house, Gwen had not even
realized that Rick Stewart had a brother. Everything else about the man who had once been
called the Prince of Entertainment was, even to
the most ignorant, a matter of common knowledge.

Rick Stewart was a once-in-a-lifetime phenomenon. For over twenty-five years he had
ruled the world of show business; he had, in fact,
to many people's way of thinking, created it. No
one disliked Rick Stewart—the man or the musi-
cian—which was a phenomenon in itself. He was
the standard by which all others were measured.
His name was a household word in every language
in the civilized world and even in a few that
weren't so civilized. His appeal as a sex symbol
had not faded from the first moment he burst
upon the scene at age seventeen to his last moments of glory at age forty-five, but the stuff upon
which he built his legend was much more power-

ful than that. He had been from the beginning, and remained to the end, the hero of both the common man and the elite. Stories of his generosity and the lengths to which he would go to keep in touch with his fans abounded, and the amazing part was that most of the stories appeared to be true. He had given a start to many of the popular successes in both the music and the corporate world today, but because of his insistence on keeping his good deeds secret, only after his death had the real power behind the thrones been revealed. Even when his fame put his life in danger from overenthusiastic fans, he refused to become a hermit, but often strolled the streets and the supermarkets and the public parks incognito, talking to the people who loved him, impulsively rewarding their loyalty with little gifts of jewelry, cars, mobile homes. There had never been, nor probably would there ever be, a man like him. Upon his sudden death in a small-plane crash the year before, a national day of mourning had practically been declared. Hundreds of thousands of grieving fans mobbed his L.A. home, necessitating the closing of all major highways leading to the exclusive estate. Candlelight vigils were held all over the world. The funeral had been an international event. Even now it was said that over two thousand visitors a day, ranging in age from six to sixty, filed past the grave site, and his home, which had become something of a living museum, had accommodated almost a hundred thousand visitors that year alone.

To Gwen it all seemed slightly macabre, one of those peculiar facets of human behavior over which she could only shake her head in helpless incomprehension. Certainly, Stewart had distinguished himself and some respect was due, but this kind of hero worship was completely beyond Gwen's understanding.

No doubt his brother had inherited the accumulated wealth of the international empire, it occurred to Gwen now, and she wondered why, with all of that at his disposal, he would choose to live in this relativley unknown corner of the northern California coast. She also wondered again, absently, what he was being summoned for.

The freckle-faced boy at the takeout window passed a large bag to her with a grin. "You got another body hidden back there?" he inquired, "or are you going to eat all this by yourself?"

Gwen returned his grin as she handed him the money. She was used to being teased about her appetite. "Just a glutton for punishment, I guess," she said. "I'm trying to see how many of these I can eat before I come down with terminal indigestion. Have a good evening."

She tossed a wave to him over her shoulder and caught his wink in the rearview mirror as she drove off. Gwen had that effect on every stranger she had ever met, which was one thing that made her so effective in her job. People just automatically liked her.

She parked under the yellow-green glow of the lot lights to consume her meal—two overstuffed tacos, a cheese burrito, a serving of enchiladas and a bag of cinnamon-flavored chips, all washed down with a large root beer—and she did not give a second thought to the possibility of all those calories going immediately to her hips. Though Gwen could hardly be described as model-thin, her five-foot-five frame was filled out very nicely, with no unnecessary lumps or bulges—thanks partly to the amount of physical activity her job required, and partly to her own tendency to put every ounce of energy she had into everything she did. Gwendolyn Blackshire tackled the world head-on with rarely a moment's thought or hesitation, and her physical appearance was only a reflection of the ebullient personality that controlled it.

Her face was round and deceptively soft and feminine-looking at first glance, but the sharpness of her nose and the surprising jut of her chin when she was determined quickly erased any illusions of malleability the casual observer might have. Her eyes were hazel-colored and extraordinarily bright, always lively and alert, and unfailing mirrors of her emotions. They sparkled with energy or danced with amusement, darkened like storm clouds that were backlighted with streaks of lightning when she was angry. Her father had teased her that her eyes were like prisms that scattered light wherever they happened to fall, and that a man could go blind from looking into her eyes. Her face was framed by a perfect bubble of glossy black hair that curved under below her ears and formed thick bangs across her forehead. No matter how much abuse it took during the day from wide, eye-shielding hats, strong winds, exertion and perspiration, her hair never lost its shape—but that was by design, not by fortune. The thick collar-length, plain-cut style was the only one that could survive the rigors of Gwen's job, and she had never regretted having to cut her long, healthy locks when she had gone into law enforcement. Her femininity had had to take a backseat to other important concerns more than once in the past few years.

She was, all in all, not a stunningly attractive woman, or a particularly plain one. She was Gwen, with a personality and a charm of her own, stormy and bubbly, impulsive and patient, head-strong and wise, and few people, if asked, could have given a better description of her than that. But few people, if any, had ever bothered to look beyond the surface for the real person who made up all the contradictions that were Gwendolyn Blackshire.

It was not quite nine o'clock when Gwen pulled her car back onto the highway, and she was satis-fied with her timing. The party would not yet have gotten into full swing, so she would not have to fight her way through the confusion of a wild ce-lebrity bash, but it was late enough so that she could be confident that the host wouldn't have run out at the last minute for a bottle of mixer or a package of chips or whatever it was they served at affairs like that. She giggled a little at the thought that she, Gwendolyn Blackshire, would be attend-ing a party to which invitations could not be bought at any cost, and she thought she might even hang around and enjoy the star-studded at-mosphere awhile before announcing herself. Ev-ery job had to have some fringe benefits, after all. But she knew that she probably wouldn't. She still had laundry to do that night.

There was no problem finding the house on Beachwood Lane, especially since it was one of only three. Immediately Gwen knew she had been somewhat off on her calculations about what stage the party would be in. The street was double-parked with gleaming sports cars and sedans of every description, and the spillover led up a curving driveway, where lights and noise spilled from a tree-shielded chalet on the top of the hill. From the size of the crowd and the sounds of the revelry, Gwen suspected with a grimace that the party must have begun somewhere around three o'clock in the afternoon and was just now getting into full swing. She shrugged philosophically as she parked her car at the corner of the street—the closest place she could find—and started toward the house. This might not be as easy as she had first planned, but it would be infinitely more interesting.

The bass vibrations of the stereo reached her when she was still a good twenty feet away from the sloping driveway; as she ascended it, whoops of laughter and feminine squeals and good-natured shouting joined the cacophony. They were obviously having a very good time. An impish grin flitted across Gwen's face as she thought what would happen if she walked into the party and flashed her badge, but, of course, she wouldn't do that. Tonight she had only one duty. She would perform it with dispatch and make a discreet exit to her own cozy little home on the other side of the tracks, spending the remainder of the evening doing laundry and watching TV, setting her hair and trimming her nails.

There was nothing cozy about this place, Gwen observed as she approached the open front door. It was one of those glamorous, modern architectural designs of cedar and glass—sharp angles jutting skyward, smooth planes dominating the sea. The front lawn, which now accommodated the overflow of slightly tipsy couples from the party inside, was a finely landscaped rock garden. Though the noise of the party drowned out the sound of the breakers, Gwen was sure that the view of the ocean from the back of the house must be magnificent. A wide stone chimney divided what was obviously a multilevel design, and as she approached the house from the side, she could see the glint of the moon on the still water of a swimming pool. *Two hundred grand, easy,* she thought. Just a modest little summer place.

Gwen smiled and waved and moved through the crowded doorway just as though she had every right in the world to do so, and it amused her when perfect strangers returned her cheerful greetings. For a moment, as she stood inside the doorway, she let herself be caught up in all the gaiety and activity, imagining what it would be like to be a guest at such a function, not a gate-crasher. It took her less than a minute to decide that this really wasn't her type of affair. Not at all.

The music was deafening—new wave, she noticed, as she restrained the urge to put her hands over her ears, not a Rick Stewart tune. The crowd was lively and colorful and, as she had suspected, dressed in everything from swimsuits to sequined miniskirts. The room was so crowded that she could not even tell how it was furnished—all she got was an impression of an undulating mass of laughing, shouting, wall-to-wall people. Someone pressed a drink into her hand and she shouted her thanks but doubted that she was heard. Someone else put his arm around her waist and yelled a friendly proposition in her ear; she handed him her drink and ducked under his arm to grab a handful of mixed nuts from a nearby bowl. A young man was dancing on top of a table, and the crowd that was forming around him was laughingly rescuing the ashtrays and hors d'oeuvres trays he was upsetting. Gwen couldn't help laughing as she popped a nut into her mouth. They were having a good time.

An encouraging roar of laughter and applause grew up from the crowd around the table, and the people standing near Gwen began to edge forward, laughing and beckoning to those behind them. Caught up in the spirit—and in the press of the crowd—Gwen found herself, in a few minutes, standing at the edge of the circle that surrounded the dancer on the table, and she saw what all the renewed enthusiasm was about.

To the heavy, soul-jarring beat of a primal rock tune, the young man was slowly undoing the buttons of his Western-cut, red satin shirt. Around Gwen a chorus of females began chanting, "Take it off, baby. Take it *off*." And the young man, grinning and obviously enjoying every moment of the attention, proceeded to do just that. His hips rotated to the music, his fingers lingered provocatively at the last button, and he shimmied his shoulders and thrust his pelvis forward as he slid the slinky garment down over his arms with all

the grace and flair of a practiced professional.
Gwen tried not to grin, but she could not stop
herself from straining for a better look with the
rest of them. In a minute she would get her business done and be out of there, but in the meanwhile there was no harm in watching the show. It
was hard to be professional and disapproving in
the midst of such high spirits, and it had been a
long time since Gwen had been to a party.

Shouts and applause swelled up around her as
the star attraction caught his shirt by the cuff,
whirled it around his head several times in time
with meaningful pelvic gyrations, and then let it
fly into the crowd. Gwen was jostled and jarred as
the women behind her jumped for the shirt; there
were squeals and the sound of ripping cloth, and
someone shouted, "Is this all we get, sweetheart?" It was joined by "What're you hiding
under those jeans, beautiful?" and "How about
some action?" And one prudent fellow laughingly
called out, "Will somebody get him down from
there before he breaks his neck?"

But the young man appeared to be in more imminent danger of succumbing to the first few sug-
gestions rather than the last one, and grinning
magnonimously, he slid his long, slender fingers
to the snap of his jeans. He was obviously riding
high and feeling no pain, and although Gwen was
usually embarrassed by the lamp-shade wearers
and the loudmouth jokers who seemed to be
indigenous to any party where anything more
potent than soft drinks was served, she found
herself unabashedly entertained by this fellow—
perhaps simply because it wasn't her party. And as

ridiculous as his display was now, it could have
been worse. At least he wasn't fat and jowly and
obnoxious, and his sweet grin and compellingly
sensual movements made it hard to be offended
by what could have, in other circumstances, been
a vulgar display.

He certainly had nothing to be ashamed of
about his body. While far from beefcake, his torso
was strong and lean, hairless and well-developed.
His waist was taut and his biceps were smooth.
There was just enough musculature to disguise
his ribs, and his skin was a healthy, pale-tawny
color, like last-year's tan. As his fingers lingered enticingly at his waistband, a female voice
shouted, "Take them off, sweetie!" and Gwen,
scanning the contours of his skintight white jeans,
thought that she really wasn't in that much of a
hurry to leave after all and that she might just
hang around for a few more minutes before making inquiries about the whereabouts of her host.

But with a mischievous wink, the young man
bent down and began to untie his shoe. Somehow
he made even that seem erotic.

He had a curiously innocent, delightfully open
face. The bone structure was delicate, the nose
narrow, and his lips were softly shaped. Reddish-
brown sideburns were cut in a neat angular pattern just below his ears and toward the jaw, adding
a touch of natural masculinity to a face that would
have otherwise been almost too pretty. His thick
hair was a little darker than the sideburns, sport-
ing coppery glints and streaks of sun-lightened
gold. It was combed away from his face and behind his ears, cut just to the collar. His eyes were a

fun-filled, sparkling emerald-green, and the stubby, sand-colored lashes added to the impression
of perpetual youth. He was what Gwen in her
younger days would have called "cute": relaxed
and uninhibited by the frivolous atmosphere, and
in his obviously liberal indulgence in whatever li-
bations were being served, he looked and acted
like a carefree little boy. But there was something
about him—maybe it was in the shape of his
panther-lithe body or the movements of his hands,
or even something indefinable in that innocent
face—that made Gwen want to take a closer look.
She wasn't usually attracted to overgrown children, but this one was worth watching.

A fresh white running shoe went sailing over
her head, to the squeals and laughter of the
women behind her, followed closely by another
shoe. A sock whirled through the air and was
snatched up by someone on the other side of the
room, and the crowd was beginning to get a little
wild. Some of the male members of the crowd
were laughing, trying to coax the exhibitionist
down, but he was completely wrapped up in his
own performance now. Gwen watched as his eyes
skated lazily over the crowd, delighting in the attention, and his fingers slowly lowered the brass
zipper on his jeans. She jerked her eyes away.

Gwen had seen men undress before; she was
impatient with the sudden flush of warmth to her
cheeks and the unexpected speeding of her pulse.
Perhaps it was simply because she hadn't really
thought he would go through with this public ex-
hibition. Perhaps it was because she really did
want to see what he was hiding under those jeans.

Firmly reinstating her professional demeanor, scoldingly reminding herself what she was there for, she began to look around for some hint of the whereabouts of her host. This was really ridiculous. It was getting late and she had laundry to do.

Firm fingers slid around her waist, and a masculine voice crooned in her ear, "What do you say we check out of here, baby?" Gwen turned in annoyance, and the dark-haired man who had first given her the drink at the door nodded with a wink toward the table. "You're not really interested in that, are you? I've seen the boy in the shower," he confided, "and believe me, it's no big treat. So why don't we..."

Gwen kept her smile pleasant but wiggled away from his grasp. "I'm looking for Scott Stewart," she explained, shouting a little to be heard over the music and the whoops of encouragement around her. "Could you point him out to me?"

The man looked amused, confused and finally a little skeptical. And then, apparently deciding that she was serious, he turned his gaze meaningfully to the other side of the room.

Gwendolyn followed his direction, but she already knew what she was going to find. With a sinking feeling, she raised her eyes toward the laughing green ones of the host.

Chapter Two

Scott Stewart was slowly, provocatively, inching down his jeans. A tiny band of tawny muscular flesh rippled erotically with the persuasive motion of his hips, then a little more, a little more. Gwen swallowed dryly and jerkily, and she did not know whether that reaction was caused by sheer distress over the fact that this was the man she would be dealing with tonight—or whether it was due, purely and simply, to the incredibly evocative images that were dancing before her eyes, within the spell of the striptease. Some of his more prudent friends were reaching for him now, trying to persuade him to come down before he made a complete fool of himself; but the far more vociferous voices urged him on. He flashed a mesmerizing grin around the room and lowered the jeans farther.

More firm flesh appeared as the white denim slithered downward over a tight abdomen, below his navel, across the smooth plane of his hips. Good Lord, thought Gwen in alarm, wasn't he wearing any underclothes? But, yes—now, riding very low on his hips and barely covering the necessities, a small scrap of red material began to appear.

"Oh, no," Gwen moaned under her breath, and the rest of the show was momentarily obscured by a lusty surge in the crowd. So much for her easy assignment and quick, unobtrusive exit. The man she had come to see was as drunk as three sailors after six months at sea and making a complete ass of himself on top of the dining table, and she was going to have to fight off several dozen overheated women just to get his attention . . . if he ever came down off that table. Well, what had she expected, anyway? It was hardly reasonable to assume that a party given by Scott Stewart, heir to an international kingdom, would be a backyard barbecue with everyone singing trail songs around a camp fire. She was lucky she hadn't walked into a full-fledged orgy, although she had no doubt that that was what it would turn into if she didn't get out of there soon.

The tone of the crowd changed from laughter to a gasp of alarm; someone shouted, "Hey, man, be careful!" and "Will you get down from there?"

Gwen craned her neck just in time to see Stewart totter crazily on one foot, with his jeans leg caught on his heel, before he careened backward off the table and into the crowd. She supposed that she let out a cry of concern, along with everyone else, as she was pushed forward; but in a moment the white jeans went sailing out over the crowd, the murmurs of alarm changed again to cheers, and Scott Stewart staggered to his feet, dressed only in red bikini underwear and a beatific grin.

He received several good-natured shoves and some, delivered no doubt by the parties upon whose heads he had fallen, that were not so good-natured. The clamorous voices mixed and mingled. "Man, you are really wasted!" "Are you crazy or something?" "Hey, does anybody have anything to get this boy straightened out?" And one man took Scott's arm and shouted over his shoulder. "Okay, folks, the show is over. Ladies, take a number! You—" he gave Scott a little jerk "—come on outside and get some air."

"Somebody stole my pants," Scott complained, and the other man pulled him patiently through the crowd. "Hey, what about my drink?"

Gwen took a breath and squared her shoulders, weaving determinedly after him. There was no time like the present—especially considering that her quarry was likely to pass out at any minute and she might not get another chance.

There were a few people on the deck, but most of them had lost interest in their exhibitionist host. The man who had taken Scott outside now pushed him firmly into a wrought-iron chair and commanded, "Sit there. Breathe."

"I'm thirsty," whined Stewart.

"I'll show you thirsty," the other man muttered. He turned away from him and lighted a cigarette.

Gwen made her way toward them, her hand on the paper inside her purse.

The noise from the house receded as one of the couples went back inside and closed the door, and with it some of the chaos that had accompanied the latest entertainment. The star attraction sprawled back in the chair, naked legs spread comfortably apart, head tilted back against the chair. He closed his eyes with a heavy sigh, and Gwen hurried.

"Mr. Stewart?" she demanded, loud enough to wake him up.

The other man looked at her curiously; the brilliant-green eyes of Scott Stewart opened more slowly. "Did you bring my drink?" he inquired sweetly.

"Mr. Scott Stewart?" she specified, as per formality, and started to withdraw the paper from her purse.

Suddenly he leaped to his feet. "It's hot!" he declared. "How about a swim?"

The deck, as Gwen had suspected, overlooked a magnificent view of the ocean, a twisting trail of narrow rock steps leading downward over the cliffs to the beach below. The pool was only a few yards away, however, and Gwen assumed that that was where he was headed when he turned. But before she could do more than open her mouth for a protest, Scott Stewart had bounded down the steps of the deck toward the cliffs.

Her first reaction was sheer irritation that he had escaped so easily, but it was followed quickly by alarm as she saw his running figure weave its way unsteadily toward the steep rock steps that sheered toward the shoreline. She turned to the man beside her. "Aren't you going to stop him?" she demanded. "He's in no condition to go in the water!"

The man glanced briefly toward the receding figure of his host and shrugged, flicking his cigarette ashes onto the wooden deck. "You know what they say about drunks," he decided finally. "He'll be okay." Then he looked at her fully for the first time and a slow, friendly smile crossed his face. "What did you say your name was?"

Gwen flashed him a look of irritation, then directed her gaze toward the rapidly diminishing figure of the man she had come here to see. "Damn," she muttered and strode away after him.

Maybe it was true, as the other man had said, that a guardian angel protects drunks and little children. Gwen caught her heel twice; she lost her footing in the dark, and the uneven stones threatened to send her plumeting down the jagged cliffs on more than one occasion, but Scott Stewart proceeded at an unhampered pace in front of her. She called out to him, but he did not stop. Swearing and muttering viciously under her breath, she hurried to catch up.

The foolhardy chase down a moonlit cliffside path was prompted by only one thing, Gwen assured herself grimly—she had no choice. With every stumbling step her irritation mounted. This was all she needed at the end of a hard day—to be chasing a drunken playboy down a dark and hazardous cliff in two-inch heels. And every time she lost sight of him, she was aware of a small catch in her chest until his lithe figure reappeared, weaving its way with cheerful confidence toward the sea. The man was a total idiot. What divine power was keeping him from missing the very next step and plunging to the rocks below? What was the matter with those people back there who hadn't tried to stop him? And worse, what was the matter with her? With every arduous step, as she felt the strain in her legs and the exertion in her lungs and the perspiration gathering around her hairline, Gwen berated herself and cursed Scott Stewart. Why should she be any more concerned about his welfare than his friends apparently were? He could damn well drown himself as far as she was concerned—after she had served him that paper.

Her shoes sank deeply into the sand just as he was sprinting toward the breakers. She couldn't help it; a shaft of alarm pierced her and she cried, "Stewart! Stop!"

He didn't even slow down.

Swearing viciously and breathlessly, Gwen dropped her purse and struggled out of her shoes. "Stewart, you idiot—stop!" The undertow was merciless there this time of year, the shoreline strewn with jagged rocks. Not even the most experienced swimmers would venture into that surf, and what was she supposed to do, stand by and watch him commit suicide?

She ran across the beach—popping four buttons on her skirt. The sucking tide dragged down her feet, and surf soaked her knees; she grabbed his arm just as he was preparing to take a running leap toward an approaching breaker. "You crazy person," she screamed at him, "what are you trying to do—get yourself killed?"

His look was startled as she shoved him backward; he lost his balance and sat down hard on the mucky sand. Gwen jumped out of the way just in time to save herself from a good soaking as a wave crashed against his chest.

The force of the wave knocked him flat—and

also appeared to have knocked a small measure of sense into him. He sat up, gasping and sputtering and wiping sand and salt from his eyes; he shook his wet hair like a sheepdog emerging from a bath, and then he looked up at her, a slow grin spreading as he registered her presence for the first time. "It's a good thing you stopped me," he admitted pleasantly. "I can't swim a stroke."

Gwen stared at him in exasperation mixed with incredulity, but he looked so cheerfully unrepentant that it would be pointless to be furious with him. "It seemed easier," she agreed dryly, extending her hand to help him up, "than pulling your body out of the tide after the fact."

He grasped her hand firmly, looking up at her with a friendly smile, an open curiosity playing on his face. "Do I know you?" he inquired politely.

Another breaker was forming, and Gwen grasped his wrist with both hands, hauling him to his feet. He stumbled against her, laughing, struggling to regain his balance as the wave broke around their calves. Gwen got a firm hold on both his arms and dragged him away from the tide line, brushing disgustedly at her damp, sand-spotted suit as she released him.

"I got you all wet," he apologized.

"You certainly did," she agreed ungraciously.

She started back to where she had left her purse and her shoes, and he followed. "Do I?" he insisted.

"Do you what?" snapped Gwen.

"Know you."

Gwen bent to retrieve her shoes and slung her

purse over her shoulder. "My name is Gwendolyn Blackshire," she replied automatically, shaking the sand out of her shoes.

"Gwendolyn Blackshire," he repeated, enun-
ciating each syllable slowly, rolling it on his tongue
like a thing of beauty. He had a strangely arresting
voice—soft, sonorous—and even in his inebriated
state the words were clear and unaffected, with
just the slightest hint of a musical drawl. Gwen
glanced at him, and an expression of dreamy-eyed
contemplation had come over his face; it was
so sweet that it almost made her smile. "I like
that," he decided. "Gwendolyn Blackshire. Castles and old velvet. A hundred candles on wooden
candlesticks. Twisting stairways and tower rooms.
What do you call that—gothic? Yes." He nodded.
"Gothic." He smiled at her. "Nice."

Gwendolyn stood before him, looking at him
carefully. "How drunk are you?" she asked clearly.

The smile widened. "Not so bad," he returned
cheerfully. "There are only two of you now.
There used to be four. But," he added gallantly,
"all of them are very pretty, Gwendolyn Blackshire."

Gwendolyn struggled with a smile. It went
against her nature to be short-tempered with
children, old people or the mentally unstable,
and Scott Stewart seemed to fall somewhere
among those categories at the moment. Besides,
he was . . . cute. Completely harmless and almost
endearing in a totally exasperating way. "I doubt
whether you can tell," she informed him wryly,
"whether I'm a male or a female." She touched

his arm to guide him toward the steps. "Come on, let's go back to the house."

"Oh, I can tell," he corrected her airily. He completely ignored her directions and flashed her an innocent grin as he turned in the opposite direction. "When I fell up against you a minute ago, I checked," he explained simply and started walking down the beach.

For a moment Gwen only gaped at him, torn between a sense of insult at his outrageous statement and alarm that he was walking away from her—and an almost overwhelming urge to laugh out loud with helpless incredulity. "Wait a minute!" She hooked her shoes over her fingers and ran a few steps after him.

She caught his arm with a gentle pressure and tried to turn him around. "The house is back that way," she explained patiently.

"I don't want to go back to the house," he replied, unconcerned. "It's too hot. I think I'll walk for a while."

Gwen fell back, staring after him. Her options were limited. Though not a massively built man, he was at least three inches taller and forty pounds heavier than she, and it was obvious that she was not going to get him back up those cliffside steps if he did not want to go. And it was also fairly obvious that the only thing he wanted to do right now was go for a walk on the beach. In the middle of the night. In his underwear.

"Oh, damn," she said angrily, and stood there for a long moment, chewing her underlip, watching him go. What was she supposed to do, serve him the paper and leave him here? That was all the law required. She would put the summons in his hand, and what happened after that was none of her business. He wouldn't even remember it in the morning. And where would he put it if she gave it to him? He wasn't exactly wearing pockets. Most likely, it would end up floating out to sea, and could she really live with her conscience if he were arrested for disobeying a court order about which he had never known anything? That wasn't her problem.

She could go away and come back the next day. And leave him here to wander into the ocean or pass out on the beach and be carried out by the tide, or to try to climb back up those steps and break his fool neck.

"Oh, damn," she said again between clenched teeth, and she hurried to catch up with him. *You're doing it again, Wendy.* Addressing herself by her childhood nickname was a sure sign she was very annoyed. *Taking the whole world on your shoulders, interfering in things that are none of your concern. This man is not your responsibility. Go back to the house and send someone from the party down for him. You don't need this.*

She came up beside him, a little breathless, and he smiled down at her. "Sure is pretty out tonight, isn't it?" He inhaled deeply of the cool, salty air. "Look at those stars." He tilted his head back extravagantly to examine them, swayed uncertainly on his feet, and laughed as he stumbled.

He clutched her arm to regain his balance, his eyes dancing gaily. "Guess I'd better not do that anymore!" he declared. "You should see how those stars are spinning around!"

"I'll pass." Her tone was dry as she placed a steadying hand on his bare back and he slowly regained his balance. His skin was warm despite the chill night, and when she touched him, a peculiar alertness came into his eyes; he suddenly did not look so drunk anymore.

"I guess you think I'm pretty disgusting, don't you?" he said softly, watching her.

Gwen was aware that her fingers were lingering on his skin, and the sensation was smooth and pleasurable. She quickly released him. "Fairly," she agreed amicably, and started walking again.

He darted her a friendly look from beneath sand-colored lashes as he fell into step beside her. "So," he inquired pleasantly, "D'you wanna have sex?"

Gwen choked with an uncertain sound, and as much as she knew she should have delivered some well-calculated, ego-slaughtering retort, she simply couldn't keep the mirth from bubbling through. How could she be angry with those sweet green eyes? "Another time, perhaps," she demurred politely.

Scott shrugged amiably and caught her hand, swinging it casually between them as he continued on his suprisingly surefooted way. The lights spilling down the cliffside slowly receded behind them; the rush of the tide began to swallow up the bass of the stereo. How was she ever going to get him to turn around?

"Gwendolyn," he said after a moment, again rolling the syllables in a delightfully languorous way. He glanced at her. "I guess they call you Wendy."

"They call me Gwen," she said, rather sharply. For years she had been working on her friends to drop the nickname she had outgrown in high school and was just now beginning to make some progress. Wendy simply wasn't an appropriate name for a twenty-seven-year-old officer of the law; Wendy was not who she was anymore.

"I like Wendy," he decided obstreperously, and to her very great annoyance, began singing the popular tune from the sixties by the same name. She pulled her hand away in irritation, and he continued singing, keeping time to the rhythm with his steps, completely unaware.

This was really ridiculous. It was cold out here and the house was getting farther away. Where did he think he was going? And what was she going to do about it? Her panty hose were ruined, and sharp particles of sand were wedging themselves between her toes. *All right, Miss Officer of the Law, do something. Whip out your badge and browbeat him back to the house where he belongs! You keep this up and you'll be halfway to Oregon before he sobers up.*

Gwen cast a frustrated look around her, blocking out the sound of his silly singing, and she slowly began to realize where they were. She had walked along the beach several times from her house to the place where the sandy shoreline ended in a rugged break of timeless boulders some distance back; she had absently observed the majestic beach castles atop the cliff and never realized that one of them belonged to Scott Stewart. She did not walk this far as a matter of course—she guessed the distance from her house to the point where they were now was about three miles — but on warm summer days it was a pleasant excursion. She doubted that it would be quite so enjoyable in the middle of the night, with the chill winds blowing off the water.

Scott stopped singing abruptly and looked down, examining his sand-encrusted feet, his naked legs, the scrap of red material around his hips. "Lord," he said a little weakly. "Am I really walking down a public beach in my underwear?"

Again, Gwen made a choking sound to subdue outrageous laughter. But this was her chance. "You certainly are," she assured him. She took his arm and attempted to gently turn him around. "Why don't we go back to the house and get your pants?"

For a moment the confused green eyes looked as though they might be persuaded, but then he smiled again, brilliantly, and decided, "No, thanks. It's too hot for clothes. I'd rather stay here."

Gwen sighed and released his arm. He walked on, unconcerned, and she trudged after him. The fresh air was bound to sober him up sooner or later, and then perhaps he would be more reasonable. Meanwhile, she might as well relax and enjoy the view.

Chapter Three

Gwen did not get as much opportunity to enjoy the beach at night as she would have liked. Usually she was too tired, or it was so late after her long drive home that she had time for nothing more than her household chores, dinner and bed. She now had a chance to see what she had been missing, and it was magnificent.

The moon was bright enough to cast shadows on the smooth, dark sand on which they walked; it turned the deep water to a mysteriously reflective hue of navy-blue that looked almost transparent. The breakers were pearly-white and translucent, dotting the distant horizon, undulating offshore, crashing against the rocks. The sky was like a sheer dark veil with tiny rips in it through which tantalizing glimpses of white fire were visible. The breeze was sharp and invigorating, lifting her hair, combing across her scalp, leaving the taste of salt on her lips. And the sound—roaring, murmuring, crashing and receding—Gwen loved the sound of the ocean. Nowhere was one more alive than on the beach, and the beach at night wove its own magical spell. It wrapped itself around something

primal within her, stroking and caressing normally
subdued instincts and teasing to life secret fantasies and little-examined emotions. The beach, the
night, were meant for lovers.

Gwen glanced at her silent companion, and she
wished suddenly that she had not stopped holding
his hand. She moved her eyes away but found
them all too soon drawn back to him. Well, he was
walking beside her practically naked—what was
she supposed to do but look? He might be a
drunkard, an overgrown child, an irresponsible
rich kid who epitomized everything she despised,
and he was certainly, all things considered, not the
first person she would have chosen to take a romantic stroll along the beach with, but he was, she
had to admit, not entirely hard on the eyes.

He carried his shoulders straight, his head back,
with an innate confidence that Gwen could not
help but admire, especially considering the fact
that, in his present state, he was likely to lose his
balance and fall flat on his face at any moment if
he did not pay more attention to where he was
walking. There was something naturally attractive
about his posture. Easy and relaxed, it empha-
sized square shoulders and smooth arm musculature; it gave his profile a slightly leonine look. The
breeze played through his hair, and he lifted his
face to it instictively, parting his lips a little to taste
the salt air. His lips would be very soft, Gwen
imagined.

Gwen let her eyes travel down his torso, un-
abashed—across the brief shield of red material,
over his lightly furred thighs and taut calves. He
was hardly in any position to object to her scru-

tiny, even if he were aware of it. He had a strong body and that surprised her. She would have thought that the indulgent life he led would have left telltale traces of dissipation—a slight sag around the waist, toneless thighs, blurred facial definition and weak biceps—but none were evident. He apparently worked hard at some gym during the day to make up for the damage he did himself at night. His legs were strong, his arms lean and naturally muscled, his neck well-corded. Shamelessly, she let her eyes wander again to the strip of material below his waist and decided that that attire showed off his best features to advantage. His buttocks were tight and well-shaped, and from the somewhat limited view she had as she walked beside him, she suspected that the derogatory comment made to her by the man who claimed to have seen Scott Stewart in the shower was far off the mark.

Gwen wished briefly that he were not quite so drunk, then dismissed her errant thoughts impatiently. It was the sea air, the moon, the sonorous rumblings of the ocean; it was easy to fantasize, and Gwen did not allow herself that harmless indulgence nearly often enough.

The sound of his voice brought her back to the present quickly and easily. "You know," he offered casually, "I don't usually do this kind of thing."

"Walk naked down a public beach in the middle of the night?" she prompted automatically and then stifled a giggle as he looked down quickly in alarm, as though trying to assure himself he was not, indeed, naked.

He grinned at her lazily, and the spark in his eyes made it hard for Gwen to remember that he probably was not even aware of her presence, much less of what he was saying. "Yeah," he agreed easily. "It's my birthday," he explained. "I was celebrating." He laughed a little. "Some people go all out for the big three-oh; that didn't bother me much. But today I'm thirty-one... really, finally, irretrievably over thirty. That's pretty important, don't you think?" He looked at her as though he really expected an answer, and she nodded soberly.

"Yes, indeed," she agreed. "High time to stop throwing away your life with both hands and settle down to some serious business."

He peered at her peculiarly. "Is that what I'm doing?" he inquired. "Throwing away my life?"

Gwen shrugged. She saw no reason to get into a philosophical discussion with this man about whom she knew nothing and, if the truth be told, cared even less, especially since he wouldn't remember a word she said in the morning. So she offered simply, "Aren't you?"

Surprisingly, he was silent. Even more surprisingly, he actually seemed to be thinking about it. After a moment, he bent and scooped up a broken shell; he held it in his hand for a moment before tossing it lightly away. "Maybe," he admitted. His voice sounded serious. "Since Ricky died, there doesn't seem to be much point—"

He broke off suddenly, and the words, the tone of his voice, his abrupt silence, hit Gwen with a mild jolt. She suddenly realized whom she was talking to. Not just a well-built body walking along the beach in his red knit bikini briefs, not just a playful boy with a head full of alcohol and not a care in the world, not just a man who was about to receive a court summons whose content she did not even know—he was Scott Stewart, a real person. A year ago nations around the world had bowed their heads in mourning for his brother, and here he was, the living legacy, walking and talking and breathing and taking on substance before her very eyes. Thinking real thoughts, speaking quiet words, feeling things Gwen did not want to know about.

She felt a shaft of irritation even as her curiosity drew her to him. Cardinal mistake: seeing the faces on the other side of the badge as real people. She wanted to grab his arm and whirl him around and send him on his way back up the cliff where he belonged, emphasizing her point with the heel of her shoe, if necessary. She wanted to finish her business and get back to her own cozy little cottage, where, by tomorrow morning, she would have forgotten what Scott Stewart looked like. What was she doing, walking down a deserted moonlit beach with him? Why did she find herself looking into that sweet-sad face and wondering what he was thinking? Why should she care?

And then he glanced at her; his smile seemed a little uneasy, embarrassed. He shrugged his shoulders uncomfortably. "I guess you think it's pretty heartless of me, having a party like this so close to the anniversary of his death."

"Stop telling me what I think," Gwen replied, more irritably than she intended. At his startled look, she gentled her tone. "I don't think it's

heartless," she said. "I don't think it has anything
to do with you at all."

He looked for a moment as though he did not
quite know how to take that, and then he started
walking again. "Fifteen thousand people," he said
softly, after a moment. "That's how many went
by the grave site last week on the anniversary day.
They still had to turn people away." Gwen wondered unexpectedly what that must have been
like. Moments like those should be reserved for
the grief of family and close friends. How would it
be to be unable to visit your own brother's grave
because thousands of strangers had prior claim?

"You must ... miss him," Gwen offered inadequately, because some expression of comfort
seemed to be in order.

"He was my whole life." Scott replied simply,
and then he smiled vaguely. "Just like he was to
everyone around him, I guess."

Something soft turned within Gwen for him.
How could she listen to that dejected tone, see the
unresolved sorrow in the gentle face, and not
want to put her arms around him and comfort
him? Who was Scott Stewart, really; what was he
feeling; how could she share it with him? *You're
doing it again, Wendy.*

As though reading her thoughts, Scott reached
out and took her hand, holding it lightly as they
walked in a warm embrace. He was silent, and she
let her fingers twine around his, sharing no more
than the moment. There was a reminiscent smile
in his voice when he spoke again. "He was really
great, you know? I mean, it wasn't all just press
stuff. He was really as good as everybody thought

he was. Sometimes—" He glanced at her, as though uncertain of her reaction. He obviously wasn't used to talking about his brother. Gwen smiled at him and he relaxed, continuing. "Sometimes he would send a bunch of us down to the bus station, our pockets stuffed with hundred-dollar bills, and it was kind of a contest to see how much we could give away without getting caught. We'd tuck bills into women's purses and little kids' pockets, hide them under baby blankets or fold them into paper towels in the restrooms. He used to love to hear our stories, and it was a great feeling, you know, to think about how some mother was going to start to diaper her baby and find a hundred dollars—probably more money than she'd ever seen in one place in her life. And those stories about him taking people off the streets and giving them the keys to a new car? They were really true. I used to go out and recruit for him sometimes. The only hard part was trying to figure out who deserved it the most—according to Ricky, everybody in the world deserved it the most."

Gwen shook her head a little, finding this all a little hard to absorb. "Sounds like something out of an old TV show," she admitted. "What was it—did he just like playing the anonymous benefactor bit?"

Scott nodded, smiling. "Partly, I guess. But most of it was just him, you know?" He looked at her almost anxiously, searching her face. Gwen realized with no effort at all that he was looking for approval from her; that he felt inadequate trying to extol the legend's virtues, and he needed some sign of reassurance that she understood. "It was just him."

Gwen nodded. She could certainly not relate to all the particulars, but the love of one brother for another was not hard to comprehend. "You must have been very close," she said.

"He was the greatest man I ever knew," Scott replied quietly, and it was a long time later before Gwen realized that he had not really confirmed her observation.

Scott ducked again to sweep up another shell from the ground, not releasing her hand, displaying remarkable agility for a man in his condition. He bounced the little shell in the palm of his hand, studying it as he spoke, effectively hiding from her his expression. "I guess you know the story," he began after a time, still not looking at her. "Growing up in the Kentucky coal mines, alcoholic father . . . a living hell is what it was. I was only six when Ricky left. That night . . ." The soft sound he made was rueful and pained; Gwen saw his hand tighten around the shell. "I can remember it like it was yesterday. We slept in this little room in back of the kitchen, about as big as a closet, with mattresses on the floor so thin that in the wintertime you could feel the wind coming up through the floorboards, and it would cut right through you. Ricky came over to me and told me he was leaving, and I remember . . ." His voice was heavy, so deep in his own memories that Gwen had to strain to catch the sound of it. Yet as he spoke the taste of the salt breeze and the sound of the surf receded, and she traveled back in time with him, back to a cramped little room tasting of coal dust and smelling of cabbage, back where two boys huddled together and whispered in the dark. "I remember I was so scared." His voice deepened with intensity; the fingers of his hand tightened slightly around hers. "Ricky was the closest thing to a parent I had, I guess, with my dad the way he was and Ma beat senseless half the time, and when he left I was going to be all alone. But then I was glad, too." A slight ferocity crept into his voice even above the note of cautious wonder. "Glad that he, at least, was getting out. That one of us was going to make it.

"I was trying to be real brave," he continued, "and not let him know how much I wanted him to stay. But I swear, Wendy, to this day whenever I think about that night I get the cold sweats. And then he came over to me, and he put his arms around me, and he promised he would come back for me. And he ... cried, you know?" He said it as though, even after all this time, he could not quite resolve that childhood memory with the image of Rick Stewart. "He held me in his arms and he was crying, and he swore that no matter what it took he would come back for me."

There was a silence as the past slowly evaporated and Scott moved painfully forward through the years. Gwen, helpless beneath the spell of his memories, could do nothing but wait for him. After a long time he seemed to settle himself into the present, and he began to speak again, somewhat more easily. "Hell," he said, tossing the shell away, "I was just a kid, but you grow up pretty fast in that kind of life, and I guess there wasn't too much I believed in. I knew Ricky

would be crazy ever to try to come back for me.
He was out of there and glad of it. I knew he was
sending us money whenever he could, but the old
man always got hold of it, so it didn't do much
good. It was less than a year later, I guess, that he
finally drank himself to death and then, would
you believe it?'' He shook his head with a soft,
still-incredulous laugh as he looked back through
time and found the memory no less wonderful
than the reality. "I woke up one morning and out
in front of the house was the biggest, whitest,
shiniest car I'd ever seen in my life. I mean, that
limo was as long as a damn cattle car. And there
was Ricky, standing in the doorway, looking like
something that just stepped down off Mount
Olympus.'' Again he chuckled. "I was about
eight, I guess, and you can imagine what it looked
like to me.'' His voice fell a little, his hand tensed
around hers. "All those days peering out that
dingy window, all those nights listening to Ma
scream while the old man beat her and praying to
God and then to Ricky until I could hardly tell the
difference between the two—I guess to me they
were the same thing—dreaming that Ricky would
come bursting through the door on a white
charger to save us all.'' He smiled. "And then he
did,'' he concluded simply.

Gwen did not know what to say. She was so
moved, so touched and torn by his pain and his
memories that she doubted whether she could
have spoken had she known the words. She was
glad he was holding her hand. Tightening her
fingers around his was the only way she knew to
express what she was feeling for him at that mo-

ment. It was inadequate, but the gesture made him look at her, and when the soft smile lightened his eyes, Gwen felt something tenuous and exploratory within her flutter to meet him.

"So," she managed in a moment, tearing her eyes away, "you all lived happily ever after."

He looked at her for another moment, then appeared to understand her somewhat desperate signal to lighten the mood. "Pretty much," he agreed. "Ricky bundled us both into that great big Cadillac." He laughed. "I remember Ma didn't want to get in because she was afraid of getting the velvet seats dirty. He swept us off to L.A. and it was Wonderland time. We didn't have any idea how successful he'd gotten to be in just two years. Even if we had, we couldn't have imagined what it was like. My room looked like a castle. I remember standing there at the door of it, bug-eyed, looking at the train sets and the shiny blue bike and the biggest bed I'd ever seen, and walls crammed full of more books and games and toys than I even knew there were in the whole world—I mean, I had never even seen a television set before, and there were two of them right there in that room. I just stood there, afraid to touch any of it, and Ricky came up beside me and knelt down and put his arm around my shoulders, and he just kind of grinned and said, 'I told you I'd come back for you, didn't I?'" Scott glanced at her quickly and gave a small deprecating smile, as though half-afraid he might have said too much or revealed too much. "So, anyway," he continued casually, "the rest is history. The finest schools, the nicest clothes, the fastest cars—Europe, island vacations, Ivy League college. Ricky didn't even finish high school, but he made damn sure I got into the best university in the country. He kept his promises, all right."

They walked in silence for a while, their hands linked, their mood shared. Gwen tried, with some wonder, to adjust to the changes that had come over her. Only a few moments ago she had been walking along the beach with a stranger for whom she felt little but amusement and contempt, a man she did not know and did not wish to know—and now she felt as though she had lived his whole life. It wasn't right. He was nothing but a face in the crowd; she was no more than an arm of the law; she should do something to put their roles back into perspective. But already she sensed it was too late for that, and the worst part was that she was content with matters the way they were. She did not want to break the gentle warmth of emotional intimacy that bound them together, two strangers on an empty moonlit beach.

She inquired softly after a time, "Is your mother still living?"

"She died about ten years ago," Scott replied. "Her last years were happy, though. Maybe enough to make up for all that went before."

Gwen nodded, looking at him. "And what about you? What did you do when you finished college?"

"Worked for Ricky," he answered, as though it were obvious. "I headed his security team."

Gwen puzzled for a moment over that. An Ivy League education hardly seemed necessary for that type of work, but she didn't pursue it any further. "And now?" she prompted.

He shrugged. "I sign papers, generally do what the lawyers tell me to." And he flashed her a quick grin. "I keep busy, wasting my life."

Gwen would have liked to retort to that, but he suddenly seemed to lose interest in conversation. He looked away from her, focusing his attention on his trudging footsteps, and Gwen felt him shiver in the cool breeze.

They had walked a long way; even Gwen was getting tired. In amazement she realized they were probably closer to her house than to his, and who knew what time it was? They were probably sending a search party out for Scott back at the house—assuming that anyone had yet slowed down enough to notice he was missing.

She stopped and tugged at his hand. He shivered again. "Come on," she persuaded, "we'd better turn back. It's late and people are probably worried about you."

He looked at her, but his eyes were unfocused, his voice a little strained. "Is it cold out here, or is it just me?"

Gwen laughed. "Both. It's cold, and you're half-naked. Here, put this around your shoulders." She started to shrug out of her jacket, but never completed the action.

"Oh, no." His voice was weak and his hand suddenly damp as he slid it out of hers and brought it rather shakily to his head. "I feel awful. I hope you won't take this personally but I think—"

He had no need to finish the sentence. He turned abruptly and stumbled a few steps away from her; Gwen's own stomach churned in sympathy for him as she heard the soft sounds of his retching.

She discreetly walked away and down toward the shoreline, digging in her purse for the scarf she had worn over her hair that morning. Her hand brushed over the legal paper at the bottom, but she ignored it, drawing out the scarf and kneeling to dampen it in the water. When she walked back up to him, Scott was sitting on the sand with his head between his knees, looking weak and shaky and thoroughly miserable.

His face was ghastly white and shone with perspiration in the moonlight, his breathing labored. Gwen felt a twist of alarm as she knelt beside him and touched the damp cloth to his cheek; he lifted his head with an effort. "Do you know," he said shakily, "those long nights when you can't get to sleep because every stupid, vile and embarrassing thing you've ever done keeps running through your head? I've just added another one to my list."

Gwen brushed his damp hair away from his face, concern tightening her own voice as she blotted his forehead with the cloth. He looked terrible. "Scott," she inquired cautiously, "you didn't take any pills or anything, did you, while you were drinking?"

Weakly he shook his head. "Just—the booze." It seemed to be very difficult for him to speak, and he was still breathing hard. "I'm not a very good drinker. After my dad, I never got in the habit—wipes me out every time. I should know better."

That long speech completely exhausted him, and he sank down onto the sand, trying for a moment to support his weight on his elbows and then giving up and lying full-length on the ground. "Weird metabolism, too," he muttered, and he seemed to be drifting off. "Just can't handle it." With one last gargantuan effort he mustered a weak smile. "I apologize," he said distinctly. "I don't usually throw up on the first date." His eyes started to close.

Oh, no. He couldn't pass out here, on an open beach, prey to all the elements... how would she ever get him back home? Torn between outrageous amusement for his behavior and sympathy for his misery, Gwen grabbed his shoulder and shook him hard. "Scott, wake up," she commanded. "You can't go to sleep now. Sit up. Talk to me."

His eyes fluttered open—sweet, innocent, totally blameless eyes. "I'm sure you're right," he said carefully. He frowned in concentration. "I'll try to talk to you, but I don't think I can sit up. The whole world is spinning around. And everything is—" he swallowed hard "—green."

Gwen sat back on her heels, unable to prevent a tight skeptical smile as she watched his struggle to stay in focus. "You don't talk like you're drunk," she observed.

"Believe me," he assured her, blinking and widening his eyes, "I'm a mess." He reached out his hand and groped for the damp scarf she still held, bringing it upward clumsily and plastering it

to his face. His muffled voice came from beneath
the material. "Wake up, old boy, get it together.
You can't pass out on the lady now—she'll never
forgive you. Lord, I'm freezing."

Gwen shrugged out of her jacket and placed it
over his chest, noticing that his skin was, indeed,
puckered with cold. And small wonder. "I feel
like I'm covering the corpse," she commented
dryly, and he dragged the scarf away from his face
to reveal a vague lopsided grin that Gwen couldn't
help returning.

He took several deep breaths, concentrating on
the cool fresh air as a restorative, gathering his
energy. "All right," he announced at last. "Sitting
up."

Gwen slipped her arm around his shoulders to
assist as he struggled to a half-sitting position, lost
his balance and almost slipped back again, and finally accomplished the feat by drawing up his
knees and wrapping his arms around them, resting his forehead on his kneecaps. "Oh," he mumbled to the ground, "everything is going in circles.
You should see it."

Gwen rescued her jacket from the sand and
draped it over his shoulders as he shivered again.
She sat back and looked at him in frank disgust.
"You are really pitiful," she announced.

"I know." His voice was muffled by his knees.
"And I was trying so hard to make a good impression."

He turned his head slowly to look at her, resting
his cheek on his knees. "Where did your arms
go?" he inquired somewhat dizzily. "It felt good
when you were holding me."

Gwen looked at him searchingly. "How much," she demanded, "did you have to drink?"

"Not much," he assured her, trying to keep his voice even and his eyes focused. "I told you, weird metabolism. Ricky didn't drink either." He sighed, more as a struggle for breath than a reflection of emotions. "That's how he got his reputation as a saint. Completely unflawed hero," he murmured, and his eyes started to drift closed again. "The kind every mother, mother's child and mother's mother could worship without fear. That was his secret, you know. There just aren't too many perfect heroes left anymore."

And what was it like, Gwen wondered, to live in the shadow of that hero? Did anyone ever think about the hangers-on, the friends and relatives of those few select people who are larger than life? What was it like for those who loved the kings and presidents and superstars of the world? It became a fascinating concept for Gwen, just as Scott Stewart himself was slowly growing three-dimensional for her. She tried to shake the feeling, but it persisted. She had known him—what, an hour? But she was starting to think about him as a complex, multifaceted character; she was starting to wonder about him; she was starting to feel involved with him. She didn't like that feeling at all.

She was surprised to glance his way and find that his eyes were open and that he was staring at her very alertly, very studiously. He said, "What are you thinking?"

Gwen was used to saying exactly what she thought, whether or not her opinion was asked,

but in this case she might have hedged. If she had
not been so certain that he would not remember
any of this in the morning, she most probably
would have. "I was just wondering," she responded, a slight, curious frown creasing her
brow, "how much of you is Scott Stewart and how
much is Rick Stewart's little brother."

Something very strangely like awareness flickered across his eyes. He seemed at that moment
perfectly cognizant, disturbingly rational. And he
held her gaze with interest. "I'm not sure," he
answered, "that there's a difference between the
two. Does it matter?"

"It should," answered Gwen slowly. "Maybe
you got so used to living your life for your brother
that you forgot who you were supposed to be—if
you ever even knew. And even now that he's
gone, he's controlling you. That's not healthy."

Quick denial shadowed his eyes, along with a
startling flash of anger. "That's not true. That's a
stupid thing to say. What gives you the right to
make a judgment like that? You don't know anything about it."

Of course, Gwen realized that he was perfectly
right; she didn't know anything about it, and she
had no right to judge, but she bristled defensively.
She had known him less than an hour, but that
was long enough to see a plain truth, and she
would not back down. "Is that right?" she challenged. "Look at you." She made a small gesture
of derision toward his figure, huddled and shiver-
ing on the sand. "You're thirty-one years old and
one of the richest men in the world, and you're
wandering around an empty beach in the middle

of the night like a lost puppy. You're head of an international entertainment conglomerate, and I'll bet you can't even name one of the companies you own. You've got a degree from one of the most prestigious universities in the country, and what are you doing with it? Do you even remember what you majored in? Do you realize," she continued intensely, her eyes narrowing as she became caught up in her speech, "how lucky you are? There are over four billion people in the world, and not one of them wouldn't kill to have what you have—money, power, prestige—and what are you doing? Partying it all away."

"That's not fair—" he began, a little dazedly, but she cut him off ruthlessly.

"You know you're not supposed to drink," she continued, disgust coloring her voice and her expression, "but here you sit, in the middle of a deserted beach in your underwear, half a step from alcohol poisoning. Why did you get drunk tonight, Scott?" she probed relentlessly. "Were you celebrating or punishing yourself? Or maybe even punishing Rick for dying? Don't you see, he's still controlling you—and you're not even trying to do anything about it."

His lashes lowered slowly, but not before Gwen saw the fog of hurt there. Immediately she was stricken by guilt. She should have left well enough alone. Here he was, cold and sick and helpless, not even in full command of his mental faculties, and she had jumped on him like a charging battalion. It was none of her business. She was being cruel and callous, and he was a complete stranger to her. *Damn it, Wendy, when are you ever going to learn?* He didn't need this from her. And she didn't need to get involved.

His face was unreadable; he appeared to be studying something intently on the ground. When he looked up, his eyes were hazy with confusion and an inner turmoil at which she could only guess. "Why do you care?" he asked softly.

Care? She didn't care. Of course she didn't care. It was none of her business, except... "I care," she answered gently, "about waste. You could be so much more than this, Scott. And that makes me sad."

Her jacket had slipped from his shoulders, and because she could see his skin prickling in the moonlight and because something about his quiet, intense gaze made her very uncomfortable, she moved to straighten it. He shivered, and she let her arms linger around him for a moment for warmth. It was just a moment, and if she felt a rush of affection with the gesture, she ignored it. If she noticed pleasure in the closeness, she dismissed it. He would not remember any of this in the morning.

She started to move away, but he looked up then. There was a tender smile on his lips that surprised her, a gentle darkening of his eyes that made her heartbeat stronger. And he slowly brought his hand up to touch her chin. "You are beautiful," he said softly.

Gwen tried to laugh it off, but she couldn't make herself move away from him. His eyes seemed to hold her. His fingers were cold, but so soft against her skin, and something about his touch tightened her throat. "You can't even see me!" she retorted.

The smile deepened, causing an intriguing spark of moonlight to gather in the corner of his eye. "I can see," he responded, "exactly one and a half of you, and if they would ever stop circling around, I'm sure both of you would be absolutely gorgeous. But..." His voice grew serious, his fingers began to travel lightly over the plane of her cheek, brushing against her hair where it curved forward, exploring the texture delicately. She fought the instinct to rub her face against his palm, to turn her lips to it. "That's not what I meant. I meant," he said simply, looking at her with such openness than an unfamiliar softening lump began to form in her throat, "that you're beautiful. You, all of you. I guess you're the nicest thing that ever happened to me, Wendy."

The sweet, unaffected sincerity in the words moved Gwen profoundly. No one had ever said that to her before. *You are beautiful. You.* What a wonderful thing to say.

She had to lower her eyes, and she knew she should move away, do something to break the spell, but just then his fingers began to move lightly down her face again, tracing the shape of her nose, feathering around her lips, and she was mesmerized. She looked up almost hesitantly, and his smile captivated her. "I want to kiss you," he said, his voice softening to a husky whisper. His eyes moved to her lips and his finger followed the direction, delicately tracing a pattern around their shape, slowly, reverently, sensuously. His finger caressed her as gently and as erotically as

his lips might have done, moving over and over
the shape of her mouth, leaving her lips tingling
and parted, her eyes wide and watching. She could
feel the strength of her heartbeat, and she could
almost feel the pressure of his lips taking the place
of his finger, and that made her breathing shallow.
But he didn't move.

His smile deepened, the lovely caress of his fingertip slowly trailed away from her lips, down the
curve of her jaw, across her throat, until it met the
band of material there, and then he dropped his
hand. "But I won't," he assured her. Though the
words were light, his voice was still throaty, and
the green sparks that lingered in his eyes gave no
indication that the fire was dying. "I'm perfectly
aware that my mouth tastes like a garbage pail at
the moment, and I don't imagine you find yourself exactly overwhelmed by my sex appeal right
now." He smiled again, more to reassure himself
than her, and his eyes were searching hers anxiously. Gwen quickly looked down, afraid he
would read entirely too clearly just exactly how af-
fected she was by his sex appeal. And he said
again, softly, "But I sure do want to kiss you."

And that was enough. Under other circumstances, maybe, but he was drunk, and it was cold
and getting late, and she had allowed herself to be
caught up far too much in his spell already. She
got to her feet. "Come on," she persuaded. Her
own voice sounded a little thick and that annoyed
her. "Time to start back."

He did not answer for a moment. His face was
resting on his knees again. *Damn,* Wendy thought.
He floated in and out of consciousness at the most

annoyingly inconvenient moments. If she had not seen for herself the evidence of his inebriation, she would have thought he was faking it all just to get her attention.

"Scott," she began impatiently, reaching down for him.

"Will you do me a favor?" He spoke suddenly, and his voice sounded odd. He did not look up. "Will you walk down to the shore for a minute?" He took an unsteady breath. "I'm going to be sick again."

For a moment she looked at him helplessly, and her whole being seemed to twist in sympathy for him. Then she turned and did as he asked.

Chapter Four

Gwen stood at the tide line, far enough from the creeping edge of foam to keep her toes from getting soaked, absently watching the shadow of a ship on the horizon. She tried to smother a rueful smile and she shook her head a little in amazement. What in the world was she, Gwendolyn Blackshire, doing baby-sitting a half-grown playboy with a vodka overdose? How had she let it go this far? Little over an hour ago and several miles down the beach she had had everything straight in her head. Her only intention had been to execute her duty in the most efficient and impersonal way possible, just as she did every day of her life, to deliver the papers entrusted to her and walk away without giving it another thought—the whole transaction should have taken less than half a minute. But here she was, out in the middle of nowhere with a stranger whose entire life story she knew, and no end in sight.

Looking up the beach, Gwen could just make out the twinkling lights that signified the beginning of her own neighborhood. And they had to turn around and walk all the way back to the other side of the beach. Gwen was tired. It had been a long day. Would he be able to make the three-mile hike back home? He'd better, she decided grimly. She wasn't about to drag his dead weight all the way down the beach and up those cliff steps. That was far and above the call of duty.

She heard his heavy footsteps behind her and she turned. He looked, if possible, even worse than ever. His face was shiny-white and his whole body sheened with perspiration. His eyes looked sunken and his hair was limp. He walked slowly and unevenly, and he was breathing hard. He carried her jacket over his arm, and when he reached her, he handed it to her and tried to smile.

Gwen had intended to deliver some light, sarcastic remark; instead, she found herself inquiring gently, "Feel any better?"

He winced. "I'd have to be dead to feel better," he replied, and it was little more than a groan. He brought his hand shakily to his forehead, pushing back his hair. "Did I apologize for this?"

"Not enough," she informed him cheerfully and moved again to drape her jacket over his shoulders. "Here, keep this on. You're going to get pneumonia."

But he shook his head. "Pneumonia sounds pretty good to me right now. I feel stupid wearing a ladies' jacket."

Gwen looked at him for a moment, her lips tightening with a dry reproval as she wondered how he could possibly feel any more stupid in a jacket than he did in his underpants; then she shrugged it off. If he wanted to freeze, it was his business. It was none of her concern, she decided firmly. She'd already done more than enough for one evening. "Come on." She jerked her head in the direction of his house. "Let's get you back home."

For a few steps he followed, unprotesting; then he suddenly stopped, looking both surprised and disoriented. "I can't walk around like this!" he said. "I'm not wearing any clothes!"

Gwen barely caught her laughter in time. Still, it sparkled in her eyes. "Brilliant deduction, Sherlock." She grabbed his arm. "Keep moving."

"But—" he stumbled a step "—what if we meet someone? I'll get arrested for indecent exposure!"

Gwen would have loved to pick up on that, but he looked so genuinely chagrined that she didn't have the heart. Sobering up was a hard business. "No one will notice in the dark," she assured him. "It just looks as if you're wearing swimming trunks. Come on."

For a moment he looked unconvinced, but he allowed her, with another gentle tug on his arm, to lead him a few more steps. Just as Gwen was contemplating the gargantuan length of beach that lay before them and wondering how in heaven's name she had ever allowed him to walk so far, he suddenly gave a cry and jerked away from her, collapsing on the sand with a string of expletives.

"Oh, for heaven's sake," Gwendolyn exclaimed in alarm. "Now what?"

He was sitting at her feet, one leg drawn up to his chest, muttering tight curses as he grabbed his calf. "A cramp," he gasped. "It hurts!"

"Oh, for—" Gwen sank to the sand beside

him, brushing his hands away, deftly digging her fingers into the rock-hard muscle of his calf in swift massaging motions. Another muffled cry escaped him. "You are really pitiful, you know that?" she scolded, irritably pushing his hands away again. "Stop that—leave it to me. It's all that alcohol in your system, you know. All your body chemicals are all screwed up. Relax, it'll be better in a minute. You need a keeper, you know that? What if I hadn't been here? You would've wandered out here and gotten your fool self killed, probably sat here on the beach till the tide washed you away."

He leaned back on his elbows, and beneath the taut lines of pain on his face a small smile began to emerge. "You're a hell of a nurse, lady," he said, and then winced and swore as she applied particularly ruthless pressure to his injured leg.

She could feel the straining knot of muscles slowly loosen with her efforts, and he gradually began to breathe easier. She had had enough of that kind of injury to know exactly how much it hurt, and again she felt her stomach tighten in sympathy with his pain. What was he doing to her, this stranger, that on less than an evening's acquaintance she was suffering when he suffered, smiling when he smiled, reaching toward him when she felt his loneliness? The shape of his calf was firm and enticing beneath her hands, slightly damp with perspiration, the hairs soft and tinglingly abrasive to her touch. She discovered that the massage had lost its remedial qualities and become more of a caress, that she was touching him and stroking him simply because she enjoyed the

feel of it, and when she looked into his eyes, the
pleasurable light of awareness there told her that
he knew it, too. She dropped her hands.

"Wendy." His voice was soft. He straightened
up and half extended an arm to reach for her.
What she saw in his eyes, in the gentle planes of
his face, made her forget for a moment that he
was ill and intoxicated, that he had caused her
more trouble in one evening than any man had a
right to. That he was an irresponsible playboy for
whom she had not an ounce of respect and about
whom she already knew more than she wanted to.
It made her forget that she was an officer of the
law and he was just a stranger in the crowd, and
that their two worlds were destined to intersect
once and only once, and that should be the end of
it. It made her want to slip into his embrace, to lay
her head against his bare chest, to feel the ocean
breeze on her face and his warmth on her body
and the surf in the background—and other even
more foolish things.

She hesitated for just a second, and even that
second was almost too long. She got quickly to her
feet and set her jaw in determined lines; she
watched the ardor in his face slowly fade to confusion as she demanded, "Can you stand up?"

He looked at her for a moment, his arm dropping to his side again. He appeared to be contemplating a great many things, among the least of
which was the question she had directed to him.
Then he appeared to come to a decision; he
dropped his eyes and used his hands for leverage
as he struggled to his feet with a grunt. "I think
so."

He put weight on his leg and Gwen saw him grimace. She caught his arm to steady him, but that didn't seem to help much. His lips were compressed tightly as he directed his gaze down the empty beach. "All right," he said, breathing hard. "Homeward bound."

After only a few steps Gwen began to despair. He was limping badly and moving at a snail's pace; every step was costing him in pain and shortness of breath. She slipped his arm around her shoulders and supported him the best she could. Even though he leaned heavily on her, the going was not any easier. "Lady," he admitted at last with an effort, "I don't know how far away from the house we are, but if it's more than a hundred yards, I don't think I'm going to make it."

That much was obvious. Gwen stopped, looking at him in a mixture of frustration and helplessness. Well, what to do now? Leave him here to freeze on the beach? Try to walk back to his house herself and send help? *Oh . . . hell.* She really didn't have much choice.

"Come on." She pushed him around and started walking up the beach in the opposite direction. "My house isn't far, just up beyond this next dune. I can call you a cab from there."

He seemed neither impressed nor concerned. He was having too much trouble just staying upright to do anything but follow her lead.

Though the distance to Gwen's house was not far by normal standards—certainly nothing compared to the distance they would have had to walk to get back to Scott's house—it wasn't an easy trek in the miry sand, half carrying a stumbling,

injured man. By the time Gwen saw her sedate
little cabin sitting offshore, nestled in sea grass
and shadowed by the moon, she was hot, sweaty
and a little short of breath. And she had never
been so glad to see anything in her life.

The only steps they had to contend with were
those leading to the front door of the stilt-
supported cottage, and those were managed with
little difficulty. The land was mostly flat on this
side of the beach, and Gwen's house sat far
enough away from the beach to overlook the
ocean without being threatened by it.

Gwen unlocked the back door and flipped on
the kitchen light with a huge sigh of relief. Scott
relieved her of his weight, leaning against the wall
for a moment to catch his breath. Now that she
could see him in the clear light of her yellow
kitchen, he did not look as bad as she had suspected, but he was still far from well. His eyes
were overbright and his forehead creased with
vague marks of pain, his shoulders lax with ex-
haustion. The exertion had put some color into
his face, but it was still shiny with an unhealthy
glow of perspiration.

"Why don't you go sit down?" she suggested,
nodding toward the adjoining living room. "Do
you want a glass of water?"

"Sounds lovely," he replied, but he did not
move immediately. His clear, bright eyes swept
around her kitchen with its sunflower design and
white enameled furnishings, the whimsical touches
in quilted potholders and ceramic knickknacks.
He smiled slowly, fascinated. "This is cute," he
said. "Not like I would have guessed at all." He

hobbled a few steps over to the table, with its yellow-and-white ladder-back chairs and yellow calico tablecloth, picking up a grinning ceramic cat whose back was stuffed with wildflowers. He laughed a little and put it down, shaking his head. "Not at all like I would have guessed."

Gwen did not know whether to be offended or not. "And just what would you have guessed?" she demanded, and then didn't even know why she cared. What was he doing here, anyway? She must have been crazy, bringing him here. But there he was, a complete stranger in her kitchen in red bikini underwear, laughing at her centerpiece. Her irritation mounted.

He looked at her thoughtfully, rather dreamily, it seemed to Gwen. The low light of fancy that had captivated her more than once this evening grew in his eyes, and he said slowly, "Gwendolyn Blackshire should live in a castle by the sea, with roses climbing up the trellises and double chandeliers in the front hall. She should wear long flowing white gowns with pearl buttons and have a black cat—a real cat," he added with a twinkle. "She should have ivory vellum stationery and heavy silver table settings with her initials scrawled in Gothic lettering on them. And a baby grand piano," he decided, then limped toward the entrance to the living room, looking for one.

Gwen shook her head, grinning, and turned on the faucet. "Just goes to show you what's in a name," she responded.

The subtle glow of lamplight from the living room informed Gwen that Scott had found the light switch, and his voice was absent as it floated back to her. "Just goes to show you why they call you Wendy," he responded.

Gwen filled a glass with water and plopped a couple of ice cubes into it. "Gwen," she corrected sternly, following him into the living room. "I told you my name is Gwen."

He did not accept the glass immediately, looking around with slightly disoriented concentration at the small, eclectically furnished room. There was a lot of wicker and brass, some low pine tables, many chairs and footstools and a single long, comfortable sofa. Everything was tied together with pastels and prints of lavender and blue, which, when the picture window was open during the day, reflected the colors of the sea and the sky. It was an airy, softly feminine room, a room for daydreams, and Scott shook his head slowly, pleased with himself. "Wendy," he decided. "Sweet and light and..." His voice grew dreamy, and even though he was not looking at her, Gwen felt herself being drawn beneath his spell. "Not quite real. Like a summer breeze or a flash of light on the water. You don't know where it's coming from or where it's going and you can't hold it—it's just there. Ephemeral." He struggled a little over the word. "But constant. Mystical, maybe. Just surely wonderful."

It took a moment for Gwen to shake herself loose from the soft amazement with which his words had captivated her. A drunk, an exhibitionist, an irresponsible child, a lost little boy, a poet—who was this man? Firmly she dismissed her softening emotions and thrust the glass into his hands. "Drink it slowly," she advised. " I'll call you a cab."

Scott accepted the water with an unsettling brilliant smile and Gwen turned quickly toward the telephone. Damn, he was making it harder and harder to remember not to take him seriously, or feel that he wasn't accountable for anything he said or did tonight.

"I'll bet," he said suddenly, setting the glass on a table, "that your bedroom is white." And then, before Gwen could make the smallest move of protest, he disappeared in that direction, toward the only other open door.

For a moment Gwen stared after him incredulously, her finger poised above the number panel, the dial tone humming in her ear. That man could move faster and with surer purpose than anyone she had ever known when he wanted to, and what in the world did he think he was doing, marching off to explore a stranger's bedroom? She shrugged and punched out the first number. That was the whole problem—he *didn't* think, and he couldn't be called upon at the moment to act like a rational human being.

She had dialed four digits when the silence from the bedroom began to grate on her nerves. "Damn," she muttered and hung up the phone. First thing she knew, he would be digging through the contents of her medicine cabinet, examining her contraceptives and feminine-hygiene supplies, and there was a limit to what she would tolerate in the name of temporary insanity. After all she had done for him tonight, the least he could do was sit here politely in the living room and not cause any trouble until his cab arrived—a cab she would end up paying for, she realized grimly, and strode off into the bedroom.

He was lying on her bed, one arm curled around her red-and-white-printed pillow sham, his cheek cushioned against its softness, his eyes closed sweetly. All men looked like little boys when they slept, their faces robbed of the cares of the day, their dreams peaceful. But there was something so heart-clenchingly innocent about this one, so utterly vulnerable and defenseless, that Gwen felt the softening spread throughout her whole body. She released a small, soft sigh of resignation. She wasn't going to call a cab. She wasn't going to kick him out in the cold with an impersonal stranger and a condemning piece of paper clutched in his hand. He was going to stay right here and sleep it off, and in the morning... well, she would deal with the morning when it came.

She moved forward to draw the coverlet over him, and he stirred. His drowsy eyes were firelit and captivating, making him for a moment appear much more alert than he could possibly be. "White," he murmured, looking around him slowly, "for purity. And red—" the edge of a smile caught at his lips and caused a flutter in Gwen's chest "—for passion. Nice."

Gwen swallowed hard and tucked the coverlet securely around his chest. "Go back to sleep," she commanded in a husky whisper. Why was she whispering? There was no one here but the two of them. Maybe it had something to do with the way his rumpled hair fell so endearingly over his forehead or the gently muscled lines of his bare shoulders. Maybe it was the way he looked at her that made it so hard for Gwen to remember that his nakedness was by accident and not design, and that kept reminding her that if they were alone together like this in other circumstances...

But these were not other circumstances. Firmly, she subdued the stirring of faint and irrational emotions. It had been a bizarre day, and she was tired. That was all it was. Scott Stewart would not remember any of this in the morning and she would forget him the moment she served her paper and sent him on his way. She had to remember that and keep her perspective on the situation.

She started to straighten up, but then he surprised her by catching her hand. He looked unnervingly sober, and that started the silly fluttering motion in her chest again. "Wendy," he said softly. His eyes searched her face with a slow tenderness that caught her completely off guard. Again she tried to fight that strange pull he seemed to have on her when he looked like that, and again she failed. "You probably won't believe this," he said, and there was a hesitant openness in his eyes that made him appear for a moment almost shy. "I mean—" a rueful smile flickered across his lips "—look at me. At us. It's been a weird night. But—" and now he grew serious again "—it's like the past year, maybe my whole life before that, was empty, and I can't remember one single good and important thing that happened to me. But tonight..." His fingers tightened slightly on hers. "With you—it was special. I'm so glad I met you, Wendy," he said simply.

Gwen felt a smile soften her features and was overcome by an almost irresistible urge to smooth his hair away from his forehead. How easy it would be to believe him.

Then he smiled and let his fingers slip from hers. "I wish I weren't so drunk," he murmured tiredly, but the meaning in his eyes was clear and explicit.

Me, too. Gwen thought unaccountably, and then she swallowed quickly the words that were almost spoken. She smiled as his eyes began to lose focus and drift closed.

"It's probably just as well," he said, sighing. "I'd probably hate myself in the morning."

"You're going to hate yourself in the morning, anyway," Gwen told him gently, but he was already asleep. For a moment she looked at him, so peaceful and innocent in his exhausted sleep, and she was reminded inexplicably of the story of Cupid and Psyche. Beautiful Cupid, god of love, betrayed by his suspicious wife while he slept...

Immediately she dismissed the foolish notion and the slight clenching of her stomach muscles that accompanied it. She straightened the coverlet around his arms, and afterward she would not know what possessed her to do it—just that he looked so vulnerable, so childlike.

She brushed his hair off his forehead and leaned down and pressed a gentle kiss on his cheek. "Good night, sweet prince," she whispered. "Pleasant dreams."

Chapter Five

Scott Stewart awoke feeling not too bad, except for the fact that a baby elephant seemed to be standing on his head and his mouth felt as if it had been recently rinsed out with hydraulic jet fuel. There were sounds of movement in the room, irritating grating and shuffling noises punctuated occasionally by the small explosion of a closing drawer or door. He had been dreaming cotton-padded fantasies about mermaids and fairies with short, dark hair and starlit eyes and laughter that sounded like clear water bubbling down a mountain cliff. The sounds of activity around him gradually drew Scott out of those spun-sugar dreams and he resented that powerfully. When he opened his eyes a crack, the white glow of morning sun was blinding, and he let out a fierce growl, flinging his forearm over her eyes.

Gwen had been awake, as was her custom, since five-thirty. She had done her push-ups and sit-ups and then had unfastened her bicycle from its security chain beneath the porch and ridden it the three miles back to Scott's house for her car. She should have resented him for that inconvenience, she knew, but the early-morning ride was so beautiful that she simply couldn't find it in her nature to be annoyed with anyone. By the time she returned to the house, unloaded the bicycle from the back of the hatchback, did another set of cooling-down exercises and put on coffee, it was almost eight o'clock. She had not even planned to be on time for work that morning, so she couldn't be upset about that, either. She called the office and told them she would be a couple of hours late, then made up the sofa bed on which she had spent an uncommonly restless night.

Gwen was in no hurry to wake Scott up, and the reasons for this were multitudinous. She was not particularly anxious to challenge the bear she knew he was likely to be with the size of the hangover he was destined for. Nor was she looking forward to lengthy explanations about who she was and how they had met and how he had ended up here. But worse, her dreams had been disturbed all night by loosely woven images of him—none of them coherent, all of them sheer fantasy—and the leftover glow of those dreams haunted her still. Last night had been a bizarre and unexpected slice out of time; isolated on a still beach and wrapped within the surrealistic glow of uncommon circumstances, they had been two different people. In the daylight hours all that would evaporate. The bleary-eyed man who would momentarily crawl out of her bed and glare at her over a possible cup of coffee would bear no resemblance to the sweet prince of her dreams. Those silly, heart-softening things he had said last night, the dreamy looks, the tug of feeling he had generated in her would hardly be real enough to be called a memory. Today she was a deputy sheriff, and he was about to be summoned for a court appearance. Today they wouldn't even know each other. Today he would leave and she would never see him again.

Gwen showered and changed into the slacks and sweater in which she would make the long drive to work, and it was almost nine o'clock. She couldn't let him sleep any longer. She really couldn't postpone the inevitable any longer. So she did not bother to keep the noise level down as she searched through her closets and drawers for something for him to wear, and when he groaned and opened his eyes, she tried to ignore the tiny catch in her chest that felt like nervousness.

"Are you awake?" she demanded cheerfully, standing over him.

Scott opened his eyes a slit and suffered unexpected disorientation as the bedroom that was not his own came gradually into focus. He had an impression of a blur of red and white and the scent of something sweet in his nostrils—perfumed soap, he thought, or a feminine dusting powder. Then his eyes slowly resolved into a concrete shape the outline of light standing over him, and Gwen's face came into view. A feeling of nebulous delight fell over him that was reminiscent of his dreams, and he murmured, dry-lipped, "So. You are real, after all."

Gwen felt a twinge of pity for him that did not completely overrule her innate sense of mischief. He did look awful, pale and puffy-eyed, his lips cracked and an untidy scruff of reddish-brown beard shadowing his lower face—but what did he expect? A man who had no more sense of responsibility than to get totally wiped out at his own party and then wander off into the night with a woman he didn't even know—in all fairness, it served him right.

He kept looking at her, foggy green eyes going over and over every part of her, and she let him, her amusement growing. Talk about your lost weekends. The questions that must be going through his head were probably driving him crazy.

He swallowed, and the effort seemed to hurt his throat. He made a weak attempt to smile. "Did I do anything last night I could be sued for?" he inquired hoarsely.

That was too much. All things considered, Gwen's mischievous streak had been tried to the very breaking point and she just couldn't resist. She sat down on the bed beside him, smiling mysteriously, and let her fingertip trail across his neck and with slow, tantalizing grace down to his chest. The way his Adam's apple jerked and his pupils dilated delighted her. "Of course not, darling," she crooned, and spread her palm over his nipple, rubbing lightly. "As long as you keep your promises." She widened her eyes innocently. "And of course you will, won't you, sweetheart?" She let her hand trail lower by just a few inches, and his skin seemed to grow heated beneath her hand. On top of a hangover, this kind of teasing foreplay could adequately be described as torture, and Gwen would have felt sorry for him if she hadn't suddenly become aware that the playful caress of her hand on his smooth, muscled chest was beginning to have a quite unexpected effect on her. She let her hand rest just over his heart, trying to ignore the tendency of her own pulse to synchronize with his strong, rapid rhythm.

He watched her levelly, obviously concentrating his entire energy on keeping his face blank and his arousal under control. And it was, also obviously, costing him a great deal. His voice was almost a croak. "Promises?"

She pretended to pout. "Surely you haven't forgotten the wedding? We set the date. After all—" and she leaned close to him, lowering her voice to a seductive whisper "—you do want the baby to have a name."

Then, to her surprise and very great consternation, a small, contented smile began to soften his face. His eyes dropped lazily, his finger came up to caress a tantalizing pattern over the shape of her jaw. "Um," he murmured. His other hand lightly circled her waist. "I've always wanted a large family. Six girls and four boys, didn't we decide that last night? I think the oldest should be a boy, don't you?" His fingers traveled a breath-stopping path around her waist and rested flat on her abdomen. There was an unsettling spark in his eye. "Do you think it's a boy? Or—" both hands now urged a gentle pressure on her back, pulling her closer "—don't you think it's hard to be sure about anything from just one time? Maybe we should . . ."

Gwen jerked away from him, heart pounding ridiculously, flustered and disconcerted. "You remember!" she accused.

"Every beautiful detail, Gwendolyn Blackshire,"

he assured her, and his eyes were dancing madly. "But I like your version better."

Gwen scowled and pushed away, her pulse racing in a tangle of confused, aftershock emotions, and she scrambled to her feet. Fortunately, Gwen was not the type of woman who blushed. "That's cheating!" she snapped at him, feigning anger she did not completely feel. What she felt mostly was the butterfly sensation of confusion and the tingle his hands had left on her skin and a peculiar pleasure with his words. "You're not supposed to remember a thing!"

He chuckled weakly and started to sit up, then fell back gingerly on the pillow with a groan. "That's an old wives' tale," he responded, once again shielding his eyes with his forearm. "Besides—" one bright-green eye peeked at her from beneath the shelter of his arm, and his voice softened "—if I had been in a coma for five years, I'd still remember you. A person doesn't forget something that important," he finished simply.

Oh, damn. Gwen stared at him in a mixture of frustration and unreasonable pleasure. This was not going at all the way she had planned. Here he was, being just as sweet and charming as he had been the night before, remembering and apparently reveling in every detail. She turned and snatched up a pair of cutoffs that someone had left there last summer. "Here," she said, tossing them to him. "I found something for you to wear. The bathroom—" she jerked her head toward the door "—is right across the hall. And hurry up, I've got to go to work."

She turned on her heel and left the room, but

she could feel those emerald eyes quiet upon her back long after she was out of range.

Gwen went to the kitchen and made as much noise as possible with the pots and pans until she heard him get up and move to the bathroom. Then she tried to relax. Okay. It was over. He was awake, sober and on his way out of her life. Another twenty or thirty minutes and the door would close forever on the brief interlude they had shared. Why did that make her sad?

Why hadn't he awakened grumpy and growling and stupidly disoriented? How had he managed to look so adorable with his unshaven face and rumpled hair, and so sexy with his long body stretched across her bed and her satin coverlet tangled around his bare legs? Why did he have to be so charming, and how could he look so damn sincere while he did it? No, this was not how she had planned it at all. The real person was supposed to be crude and shallow and thoroughly disagreeable. He was supposed to be nervous and embarrassed and uncomfortable; she was supposed to be smug and superior and completely in command. Their relationship this morning was supposed to be brisk and impersonal. But he had smiled at her and her heart started to melt; he had teased her and made her wish he wasn't teasing. He refused to pull the curtain over the illogical closeness that had begun to develop between them last night, and he made it impossible for her to forget, too. She was the one who was nervous and embarrassed, and she had done absolutely nothing to be uncomfortable about—except, perhaps, let him get a little too close. And she intended to put an end to that without delay.

Thus resolved, she did not even turn around when she heard the soft fall of his bare feet against the linoleum. She could feel him standing at the doorway, watching her, and she concentrated all of her attention on the bowl filled with eggs that she was beating within an inch of their lives. Silence drew out, stretching on her nerves, and he just stood there, watching her.

At last Scott said, "I took a shower. Hope you don't mind."

"Of course not," Gwen replied crisply, pouring the eggs into a heavy-bottomed skillet bubbling with butter. Still she did not look at him. What was this? Gwendolyn Blackshire didn't have a cowardly bone in her body. Why should one mildly good-looking drunk suddenly make her feel like a trespasser in her own kitchen?

Scott entered the room slowly, almost cautiously. He remembered it from the night before. It had made him smile then, as it threatened to do now. On the sunshine-yellow wall above her stove were the black eyes and whiskers of an enormous cat; the frilly white priscilla curtains were printed with yellow butterflies. The small table and chairs were bright-yellow lacquer with white vinyl seats. There were calico placemats on the checkered tablecloth. Every room in the house reflected a different facet of her personality: serene, passionate, whimsical, with hints of hidden underlayers that tantalized him to discover. This morning he was seeing another side of her, and that was why he moved cautiously.

Scott had awakened with the memories of the night lingering over him like an enormously powerful daydream, and she had been there, standing over him. Close enough to touch. He had wanted the dream to last; he had wanted to spin it out to its fullest potential. And he had seen the shutters come down over her eyes. It was confusing.

As he stood under a stingingly hot shower with his head ringing and his eyes aching and visions of the night jostling for attention with the unpleasant details of a hangover that should have killed a man twice his size, reluctant reality began to win out. She was upset with him. Why shouldn't she be? He groaned out loud when he thought about how she must have seen him last night. Here he was, an utter stranger, barging into her house in his underwear and passing out on her bed. He was embarrassed. There was no other word for it. But Scott's philosophy had always been to ignore unpleasant things that could not be changed, and there was no point dwelling on the fool he had made of himself last night. He hoped she would be as generous with him as he was being with himself, but he doubted it.

There were other things. His head felt like an overstuffed sock and his stomach was churning. The smells coming from the kitchen were almost his undoing. His whole body ached, and there was a knot in his right calf from the cramped muscle that made it hard not to limp. How far had they walked anyway? The lovely warmth that had been between them was gone, and he was almost worried that he might have imagined it. He thought it might just be easier to creep out the back door and

never face her again. Her back was ramrod-stiff.
She probably despised him. All the things he
wanted to say to her caught in his throat. And the
shorts she had given him to wear belonged to
another man.

Gwen scooped up six strips of crisp bacon, sparkling with grease, and spread them on a paper
towel to drain. She turned out a huge bowl of
fluffy eggs and set both dishes on the table before
him. Scott flinched and swallowed down nausea.
"There's coffee on the counter," she said, turning to remove a pan of muffins from the oven.
"Help yourself."

Coffee. That sounded like something he might
be able to keep down. Scott got up and moved on
catlike feet toward the coffeepot, careful not to jar
his head. Gwen emptied the muffins into a basket
and let the pan fall with a clatter into the sink. The
muffins were apple and smelled sickeningly sweet.

Scott said, carefully filling a mug to the halfway
mark, "Listen, I'm sorry about the inconvenience." He made himself look at her. "Last
night and all, and letting me sleep here—that was
nice," he said inadequately.

He was doing it again. Getting to her. An apology was the last thing she had expected, especially
one delivered so haltingly and earnestly. Gwen
turned away quickly, shrugging it aside as she
took plates down from the cabinet. "No problem.
I double as a foster mother for stray drunks and
lost boys." Then she winced. Had that sounded as
cruel to him as it had to her?

She didn't have the courage to look at him and

find out. She busied herself with napkins and silverware, and there was an awkward silence as he went back to the table.

He looked at her anxiously as she set a plate and silverware before him. "I hope you didn't go to all this trouble cooking breakfast just for me." He tried to hide his distaste for the steaming dishes of multiple colors and odors on the table before him, but his voice sounded a little sick as he added, "I don't usually eat breakfast."

She lifted an uninterested eyebrow and went for the butter. "You should. Solid food is the best cure for a hangover."

"Not this one," Scott assured her weakly.

"Suit yourself." She sat across from him with a mug of coffee and began enthusiastically to butter two muffins, one after the other.

Scott watched her pile most of the eggs and four strips of bacon on her plate, and then he had to distract himself or leave the table. "Where did you sleep last night?" he blurted, because that was the only thing he could think of to say.

An unexpected twinkle sparked in her eyes, and Scott felt it spread over him like a warm bath. That was how he remembered her, smiling, teasing, eyes reflecting light, scolding or disapproving, but lively and energetic—not distant and cool as she had been so far this morning. He relaxed, welcoming the gradual but irrefutable orientation of the world again. And she said, "Where do you think I slept?"

His slow grin filtered through, and it didn't cause him nearly as much pain as it should have.

"Like I said," he answered easily, his eyes sweeping her once and trying not to linger with too obvious delight on everything he saw, "don't I wish."

Gwen lowered her eyes to her coffee mug and quickly took a sip. There he was, looking so cute and natural that it was almost impossible not to relax and flirt with him a little. Gwen's most difficult role of all was the one of competent superiority she sometimes had to affect on the job. It went against her nature to be cool to people and what was the harm, really, in being friendly to Scott Stewart? Friendly did not necessarily mean accessible. And she could just ignore how sexy he looked sitting bare-chested at her kitchen table, with the damp ends of his hair curling around his ears and shower moisture glistening on his sideburns. *Admit it, Gwen, he's easy to relax with. He practically bared his soul to you last night, no use pretending he's a stranger now. Relax and enjoy it.*

She took another forkful of eggs and replied offhandedly, "Sofa bed. I'm used to overnight guests. Are you sure you don't want some of these?"

But Scott ignored her question and directed his attention to her last statement. "You are?" He kept his voice casual, but a slight twitch of one eyebrow betrayed him. "I suppose these pants came from one of your overnight guest, then."

Gwen couldn't help being amused. He sounded so pompous and self-righteous and was trying hard to sound neither, and the circumstances under which he had ended up in her bed left very little room for disapproval on his part—a fact he undoubtedly knew, but was trying to ignore.

Gwen replied with a shrug, biting into a strip of bacon, "Some of my guests arrive without pants, some of them leave without pants. Works out quite well, actually."

He did not have the grace to look embarrassed. His sense of humor was not exactly as Gwen remembered it. A line formed between his eyebrows and the color of his eyes seemed to deepen a shade. He said, "So what are you—married or living with somebody?"

It wasn't what he said, but the way he said it. As though he were actually accusing her of something—as though he had the *right* to accuse her of something. Gwen finished off her eggs and thought about not answering. There was absolutely no reason to let this irresponsible playboy, who had no business in her life at all, upset her digestion. He had already done enough to ruin her day already. She should just ignore him.

But she found, after all, that she couldn't ignore him. She said evenly, "What makes you think I have either a husband or a boyfriend? Did you see a man lurking around here ready to blow your head off last night? And what business is it of yours, anyway?"

He dismissed it all with a careless sweep of his hand and the scowl only deepened. "He could have been out of town or something. And I guess I do have a right to know whose shorts I'm wearing," he continued belligerently, "and who you're sleeping with when I'm not here."

Gwen gaped at him. There was no longer anything cute about this—it was downright insulting. How dare he suggest that her morals were deserving of censure, and what business of his was it, anyway? She gulped once on words of scathing derision that were too tangled to be formed, and she pushed up from the table, striding over to the refrigerator.

"And aren't we the smug one," she flung over her shoulder, sloshing a measure of orange juice into a glass. "Mr. International Jet-setter himself, with your orgies and your little red pills and your hot tubs and nude walks on the beach!" She gulped down the orange juice in almost one swallow and turned to him, her eyes narrowed. "So tell me, Mr. Scott Stewart, who was the last woman you slept with? Do you remember her name? Or do you take on more than one at a time?" She tossed down the rest of the orange juice and flipped her hair behind her ear as she deposited the glass with a clatter in the sink. "Spare me your self-righteous tone and your dirty little mind if you will, please—it so happens I have *nothing* to be ashamed of, and the last person I have to explain myself to is you!"

Scott winced. He knew he had blown it the moment the words were out. The last thing he wanted was to make her angry, and the last thing he needed was a shrill voice yelling at him. He knew he should apologize, but he felt compelled to defend himself. "That party last night," he responded, deliberately keeping his tone quiet, "was the first one I've given since I've been here. I moved here for the isolation, and that's exactly what I've had. I don't have any little red pills or hot tubs, and I am not, nor have I ever been, an international jet-setter. As for the last woman I slept with—'' Gwen felt herself growing uncomfortable under the steadiness of his gaze "—I don't kiss and tell, but I do remember her name because I was engaged to her at the time."

Damn. How had he turned it all around and made her feel guilty? And why did he just sit there looking so open and vulnerable, never once taking his gaze from her? Gwen marched over to the table and began clearing the dishes. She tried not to squirm under the quiet force of his eyes. This had gone on long enough. She had to get him out of here and start forgetting about him. She had to remember the only reason she had gotten involved with him in the first place was sheerly through the execution of her duty, and she had done everything but execute her duty since she had met him. Well, almost everything, she amended silently, and then to her very great consternation felt something that was almost like a flush creeping along her throat.

Scott took a sip of his coffee, hardening his features against an automatic grimace. He was used to taking it much weaker. "I'm sorry I insulted you," he offered simply, watching her and waiting for her to turn around. "All I wanted to know is whether or not you're involved with someone."

Gwen did turn around, mostly because there was no other way she could avoid it without looking foolish. A tangle of confused emotions played across her face. Why should she tell him that? Why did he want to know? What did she care if he thought she was an adulteress or morally lax—or a hooker, for that matter? Nothing had happened between them last night; anyway, he was making entirely too much of a big deal out of this. She would never see him again. It was none of his business. And he was just sitting there, looking so sober and earnest and cautiously expectant.

"The shorts belong to someone who was at a beach party here last year," she mumbled uncomfortably and crossed rather stiffly to the counter to unplug the coffeepot. "People always bring a change of clothes when they're going swimming." She took a short breath and turned to him. "And I'm not married," she added, somewhat defiantly.

It annoyed her more than she wanted to admit to see that soft, enchanting smile lighten his features. It was the kind of smile that could go straight to the heart if one were not careful. "Good," he said simply. "When can I see you again, Wendy?"

Oh, no. She should have seen it coming. She had seen it coming; she just hadn't tried very hard to avoid it. He didn't want to see her again. He would never want to see her again when he found out who she really was. She wondered suddenly and inexplicably what had happened to the woman he was engaged to, and she almost asked him. *Oh, damn.* How did everything get so complicated?

She said brusquely, "Come on, I'll drive you home. I'm late as it is."

If he noticed the change in her manner or her refusal to answer his question, he was wise enough to disguise his reaction. He followed her silently to the car and he seemed relaxed, at ease, unconcerned about anything. That bothered Gwen. He should have said something. Didn't he wonder what she was doing at his party? Didn't he care who she was or how she had happened to wander into his life? Wasn't he going to pursue the point of when they could see each other again? The idiot didn't even comment on the presence of her car or wonder how it had gotten back there, or even care that she had ridden her bicycle at six o'clock in the morning all the way to the other side of the beach to retrieve it. Wasn't he going to try, even once, to make a pass at her?

They were about a mile down the coastal highway when he spoke. Then it was only to ask, "Where do you work?"

That was her chance. All she had to do was say, "Paos County sheriff's department." And pull out the paper that was still hidden in the bottom of her purse. It would be over.

She replied tersely, "San Simon."

"Long drive," he commented.

She nodded and made no reply.

She pulled up in front of the sloping driveway that led upward to his house, and both of them noticed that at least a dozen of the cars that had been parked along the driveway and street were still there. Scott grimaced and said, "Looks like a few people didn't make it home."

For a moment Gwen felt a twinge of sympathy for him, having to go into the wreck of his house and forcibly evict leftover bodies after the night he had had. But it served him right. That's what he got for throwing wild parties and leaving in the middle of them. It was none of her business, anyway.

Scott opened his door and turned to her, smiling. There was a serene gentleness in his eyes that made them look sun-kissed, and despite the puffiness and spidery red lines, utterly captivating. "Thanks for everything, Wendy," he said simply. "I'm awfully glad I met you." Then his hand lifted, as though to touch her cheek; Gwen knew this was the moment he was going to kiss her. He would kiss her and say something beautiful and heartrending and make her believe him, make her forget everything except what he wanted her to remember.

She lifted her face infinitesimally; his hand fell back. She ignored the slight flicker of confusion and disappointment that crossed his eyes, and she said, "Better get inside. Looks like you've got your morning cut out for you."

He smiled again, undisturbed. "Sure does." He hesitated just a moment before getting out of the car. Gwen refused to meet the look she knew would be on his face. "I'll see you soon, Wendy." he said softly.

He was standing on the street, preparing to close the door, when Gwen finally got the courage to reach into her purse. "Scott," she called and leaned across the seat toward him.

He bent down to her, a look of cautious expectation on his face. And her next move was the hardest thing Gwen had ever done in her life.

Gwendolyn smiled and presented the paper to him. "Happy birthday, Scott," she said.

If she lived to be a hundred, Gwen would never forget the look on Scott Stewart's face as she

drove off; he was standing there in the street with
the wind lifting his hair and the morning sun playing on his skin, staring in uncertain puzzlement at
the official document in his hand.

Chapter Six

"All right, lady. Freeze right there."

Gwen lost her breath as something hard and round stabbed into her ribs and a heavy arm circled her throat. For a single paralyzing second every terror she had ever known flashed through her head, crowding her vision like an ever-narrowing tunnel, and she couldn't move, she couldn't scream, she couldn't even think what to do. A cold band of moisture choked her from her stomach to her solar plexus and she had no muscles. She was drowning, slowly suffocating in a sea of mindless panic, and this was it, the moment she had lived all her life in dread of, the time when she must do battle with the faceless demon of her nightmares, with nothing for protection but herself, and she was going to lose.

It was only a second. It never lasted more than a second. Of course, a lot could happen in a second. A bullet fired from a .357 could travel over a hundred feet in a second. A knife could open the jugular in a fraction of that time. A well-executed roundhouse kick could disable its victim in three-quarters of a second. The thin line between life and death could be severed in a multitude of ways, almost quicker than the deed could be planned.

But not this time. It wouldn't happen this time. Swiftly Gwen's hand came up and seized the middle finger of the fist that pressed down on her throat, snapping backward in a quick motion that startled a cry in her ear. The length of pipe he had pressed into her ribs clattered to the floor. A half-step changed their positions, and Gwen drove her boot hard into the back of his knee. Her assailant was on the floor before her, gasping and choking on expletives, and Gwen was standing above him, breathing hard and pushing back adrenaline and staring in mounting chagrin at what she had done.

"Gee, Mickey, I'm sorry!" She moved to kneel beside him but he brushed her away angrily. "Are you all right?"

"Dammit, Blackshire, I think you broke my finger!" he flung back, his face twisted with a comic mixture of surprise, fury and pain. "What the hell did you kick me so hard for?"

A group of officers was beginning to gather around them in the reception area, their faces reflecting reluctant mixtures of amusement, concern and relief that, this time, it hadn't been one of them. Someone commented, "You're lucky she didn't have better aim. You could've lost something more important than a leg."

And another said, "I warned you, Mick, the lady has the kiss of death."

"Kick of death is more like it," somebody else commented, chuckling and reached down to help Mickey up.

But Gwen was not amused. This kind of horse-play was common around the office and she was used to it. She knew part of it was because she was the only woman on the team and she was constantly being required to prove herself. She didn't mind that because the other part of it was that at any given moment any one of the men could be trusting her with his life, and they needed, for their own confidence and hers, to make damn sure she could be depended upon. That was good for Gwen, and she viewed the half-playful challenges as minitraining exercises. But in a training exercise one did not try to cripple one's partner. It was only playacting, and all that was required of her was that she break the hold or establish a standoff or otherwise prove that she could get the upper hand. There was no excuse for her letting herself get out of control that way.

Her eyes darkened with anxiety as she stepped forward. "Really, Mickey, I'm sorry. I don't know what got into me. I wasn't thinking, I guess. Here, let me look at your finger."

For a moment Mickey glared at her, then, seeing the genuine shock on her face, he reluctantly spread his hand for her.

Tim passed by on his way to the door. "Serves you right," he said severely, though he, too, was trying not to smile. "You know how Matt feels about this kind of crap. One of these days she's going to pull her piece and shoot on reflex, and then we'll all be laughing, won't we?"

"Ah, hell," one of the men defended righteously, "you know we never pull anything when she's armed. That would be crazy."

"Crazier than this?" Tim retorted, and that only made Gwen feel worse.

The finger wasn't broken, thank God, just a little pulled. Gwen could only hope Mickey didn't lose any time from work because of it; they were shorthanded enough as it was. "I'm sorry," she offered again, inadequately, but very, very genuinely, and Mickey softened as he retrieved his hand. It was hard to stay mad at Gwen.

"Forget it," he said gruffly and bent to rub the back of his leg as he hobbled off. "You just remember I owe you one!" he flung back over his shoulder, but Gwen knew she was forgiven.

Unfortunately, his forgiveness did not make her feel much better. It all boiled down to one thing: She hadn't been thinking. Her mind simply wasn't on her work. There was no more terrifying realization for a person in a job like Gwen's.

Unlike those of many modern sheriff's departments, the functions of Paos County deputies included far more than serving subpoenas and administering bench warrants and writing out tickets. Though the police departments in some of the outlying towns took a great deal of the burden off them, for the mostly rural district surrounding the county seat of San Simon, the sheriff's office was the only law enforcement agency in existence. They patrolled the highways; they responded to burglaries; they investigated murders, rapes and assaults. Every time they walked in to arbitrate what was so euphemistically termed a "domestic incident," they knew they were taking their lives into their hands, and the same was true each time they stopped a speeding motorist. Every moment of every working hour they had to be at top efficiency, every sense alert, every ounce of concentration devoted to duty. They had to be constantly ready to expect the unexpected. A moment's straying—like the one Gwen had just experienced with Mickey—could prove fatal.

Tim tossed her jacket to her, and Gwen caught it before her face. Perfect reflexes. She tried to cheer herself. At least she had reacted to Mickey. Overreaction was better than no action at all. In other circumstances her behavior would have been perfectly appropriate, even laudable.

"There's a good hockey game on tonight," Tim invited, standing with his hand on the doorknob. "Want to come over and watch?"

Gwen scowled. The trouble was that these weren't other circumstances. If she had thought about it even for a minute, if even part of her mind had been on where she was and what she was doing, she would have realized than an incident occurring at the end of shift in the middle of a crowded sheriff's office could hardly call for life-or-death techniques; she would have recognized Mickey's voice or scent or the weight of his hold. . . .

Tim lifted an eyebrow. "You don't have to look so thrilled."

Determinedly, Gwen shook herself out of it. Over. Done with. She would do better tomorrow. She pulled on her jacket and responded, "The Bruins?" She didn't really want to go home tonight. And that, of course, was the basis of the problem. She hadn't wanted to go home for the past three days, half afraid, half anxious, that the door bell would ring. She flipped her hair behind her ear and firmly blotted it out. "Let's stop and get a pizza on the way over, okay?"

Tim grinned, holding the door for her. "One extra-large pan-crust with everything coming up."

Tim knew Gwendolyn better, perhaps, than anyone in the world, and he knew exactly what was bothering her. Waiting for his 1977 Chevy to warm up in the parking lot, he said, "Did anybody ever tell you that you take yourself too seriously sometimes?"

Gwen glanced at him slyly. "Only about a million times. And as I told you every one of those times, the only thing I take seriously about myself is my failings."

"Your nobility puts me to shame," Tim murmured, and slid the car into gear. He flexed his cold fingers on the steering wheel. "So what if you're not perfect? It could be a real boost to morale around here if you weren't."

"You know the old saying," Gwen replied. "A woman has to work twice as hard as a man to prove she's half as good—fortunately, it's not hard to do." And then she shrugged, casting him a quick grin. "Besides, I don't know whether I'm perfect or not. So far, I've never had to put it to the test."

Tim groaned.

Gwen was glad Tim was too tired to pick up, as he generally would have done, on the nuances behind the last statement. It startled Gwen that she had even said it, because there was an underlying depth to the light observation that she did not want to discuss with anyone, not even Tim. It was something she rigorously avoided thinking about, except at times like these, when something happened to make her doubt her own competence.

"You have been a little drifty lately, kid," Tim said negligently, trying to disguise his own curiosity with shaded eyes. "What's up?"

"Spring fever?" Gwen suggested. "Don't forget the pizza."

Tim swung the car into the takeout pizza place and switched off the engine. "You know what Annalee thinks, don't you?" he said, jauntily pocketing the keys as they got out.

Gwen grimaced. "Since when do I care what Annalee thinks?"

"Since maybe she's right," Tim baited her cheerfully, and Gwen scowled.

The trouble was, of course, that this time Annalee might be closer to right than she knew. Of course, she insisted, with her usual flair for drama, that Gwen was in the throes of a hard-and-heavy love affair. Why else would she be so absentminded and preoccupied, so vague and unsociable? Why else, Annalee declared with glee, would she absolutely refuse to talk about her meeting with Scott Stewart?

Because the man was entitled to his privacy, Gwen had snapped back. Because there was nothing to tell. Because she hadn't even noticed what the inside of his house looked like and, she evaded uneasily, he hadn't spoken a word to her when she handed him the subpoena. Of course, she gave no hint that she had seen the mysterious personage in his underwear, that they had spent a whole evening talking, and that he had ended up in her bed. Yes, she hedged, the house was pretty luxurious. What did you expect from a guy with his kind of money? And she supposed he was fairly good-looking. She hadn't noticed a family resemblance. And, of course, Annalee read everything into her evasions that should not have been there, and her perception irritated Gwen.

She was only halfway close to the truth. It wasn't a love affair that was on Gwen's mind, but it was a man. The man was Scott Stewart, but not for the reasons Annalee supposed. And Annalee had conveniently overlooked one important piece of evidence: A woman in love flitted through her days glowing and singing and hurrying to get home every night. Gwendolyn wandered around with a scowl on her face and assiduously postponed going home for as long as she could. Those were all the signs of a woman, not in love, but suffering with a guilty conscience.

Tim was right. She did take herself too seriously. Hell, she was just doing her job; it wasn't her fault that Scott had complicated matters, and it certainly wasn't her responsibility now if he felt she had deceived him. But it bothered her. She had to be honest about it. She hadn't exactly been the perfect professional that night. She hadn't been imperfect, she defended herself righteously, but it might have been better if she had kept up the calm, impersonal reserve she had always donned when she was on the job. Perhaps she had encouraged him to feel at ease with her, had done something to invite him to confidence. For he had confided in her. He had felt close to her. And, dammit, she had to admit it to herself, she hadn't done anything to discourage him. She had felt close to him, too. Up until the very last minute she had still been holding out some secret fantasy that they would see each other again.

He was a special kind of person. Drunk or not, shallow or sincere, he intrigued her. It was simply that it was a rare thing to learn so much about one person in a single evening, to have anyone open up as Scott had done to her on such brief acquaintance. There were things she tentatively liked about him. There were more things she wanted to know about him. He touched her on some little-known and completely inexplicable level, and that in itself was a hard thing to turn away from. And if it was sheer sex appeal she was looking for, she could have done far worse. Under other circumstances... Yes, it was a hard thing to confess, but had they met under other circumstances, she would have made certain they saw each other again.

That in itself was not easy to adjust to. Given all the facts, Scott Stewart was not at all the type of man she was usually attracted to. For one thing, celebrity, even secondhand, held no appeal for her. His life-style went against everything she stood for. She did not like exhibitionists, and she was enough of an extrovert herself that she generally found it hard to get along with people of the same temperament. Obviously, their values were poles apart, and things like that were important to Gwen when establishing an initial rapport. In a nutshell, Gwen liked strong, husky, bearded men with sensitive eyes and sturdy pickup trucks. Nothing could have been further from a description of Scott Stewart.

But sometimes the things he had said drifted through her head like dandelion fluff on a summer breeze. *Castles and old velvet. A hundred candles on wooden candlesticks. You are beautiful. All of you. I guess you're the nicest thing that ever happened to me, Wendy.*

And then the memories would grow entirely too uncomfortable, and she firmly pushed them back into the recesses of her mind where they belonged, wincing a little as she did so. Poetry. Silly nonsense words that he could not possibly mean. *I sure do want to kiss you.* Gwen was used to dealing with people in a simple, straightforward manner: yes or no, black or white, just the facts, ma'am. How was she supposed to know when someone as practiced as Scott Stewart undoubtably was, was playing games? Sure, he seemed sincere. A lost little-boy act designed to get her sympathy. Of course, he spoke prettily and handled his eyes like aphrodisiacs . . . that was the way men like him operated. He probably had a bagful of tricks she had never even heard of before. Here she was feeling sorry for him when, if he had not been too drunk to perform that night, she would now be only another scalp on his belt whose name he did not even remember.

And she did not believe any of that. Not for a minute.

She avoided going home at night because Scott Stewart lived just down the street. Because she was half in dread, half in hope, that she would open the door to a knock one evening and find him standing there with hurt and accusation in his eyes, demanding an explanation. And because she knew perfectly well that if ever she got home before sundown she would start on an aimless stroll down the beach, and before she knew it, she would be standing in front of the jagged cliff steps that led up to a rambling cedar beach home. And that she might stand there for hours, just looking at it, wondering what he was doing, wondering what he was thinking, wondering if he was alone. Or worse yet, that she might begin to climb those steps.

What Gwen truly believed was that Scott Stewart probably hated her. Gwen was not used to feeling animosity from people, even when she wore her badge, and that disturbed her. Even less common was the almost certain conviction that she deserved it. And less than four hours later, she found herself telling Tim about it.

Gwen was lying on the plump, well-used sofa in Tim's one-bedroom apartment, her shoes off, her feet flung comfortably over the back. The television flickered the red-and-white cacophony of the final score and a crazy mob, and Tim lay on the floor before it, his head propped up by a seat cushion he had robbed from the easy chair. Scattered over the coffee table and floor between them were an empty pizza box, a bag of crumbled Cheetos, an open can of peanuts and a half-filled bag of nacho chips, along with six empty beer bottles. Tim reached up to lower the volume on the television as the local news was forecast, and he glanced around him with a groan. "Your stomach must be lined with stainless steel," he complained. "How can you eat so much?"

Gwen lowered her feet to the floor and began to sweep up beer caps and crumbs, stuffing empty packages and other miscellanea into the beer carton. "I was preoccupied." She shrugged. "Besides, I didn't eat any more than you did."

Tim gave a single dersisive "Ha!" and pushed himself to his feet, gathering beer bottles into both arms. He dumped them into the kitchen trash can with clinking and clattering, and called back, "You were preoccupied, maybe, but not with the game." He appeared in the doorway, casting her a shrewd look. "What's on your mind?"

"Greek mythology," responded Gwen absently, recapping the peanuts. He took the peanuts, the leftover nacho chips and a handful of trash from her with a perplexed look, and Gwen explained, "Cupid and Psyche. Remember when we studied it in school?"

"I must've been absent that day," he said, shrugging, and disappeared into the kitchen again.

When he returned, Gwen was sitting on the sofa with her arms wrapped around her knees and her chin resting on them, staring at the television set with no volume. He sat down beside her and put his arm around her shoulders, drawing her back to him. She relaxed easily against his shoulder. "Okay, babe," he invited, "tell me about Cupid and what's-its-name."

"Her," corrected Gwen. "Her name."

"My apologies. Go ahead."

"Okay," began Gwen thoughtfully. "It's actually a variation on the story of *Beauty and the Beast*—you know that one, don't you?"

Tim nodded sagely.

"Well, Psyche was this princess who was so beautiful that she made Venus, the goddess of love, jealous. So she sent her son, Cupid—"

"The little fat kid with the diaper and arrows, right?"

Gwen gave him a withering look. "The god of love," she corrected archly. "A beautiful young man in his prime." With chestnut hair and auburn sideburns and sea-green eyes, she thought, and then determinedly went on. "Cupid was supposed to go down and fix it so that Psyche would fall in love with some ugly man who would ruin her life, but he ended up pricking himself with his own arrow, and to make a long story short, she ended up marrying him. Of course, he was wonderful, perfect, and she was madly in love with him. The only thing was that she was never allowed to see him. Everyone told her that he was a monster who was so ugly that even looking at him would turn her to stone or something." Perhaps Gwen was mixing her myths, but it hardly mattered at that point. "So he only came to her at night and they made mad, passionate love, and during the day she had a palaceful of servants to wait on her, with every comfort you can imagine. He would leave her such marvelous gifts and say such beautiful things to her that Psyche really couldn't believe he was an ugly monster . . . but still that little doubt nagged, you know? She asked him why he wouldn't let her see him and he made her promise never to try; he made her promise to trust him. Eventually, of course—" Gwen shrugged "—her curiosity won out. One night while he was sleeping, she got a lamp and a knife—just in case he really turned out to be a monster—and she lighted the lamp to look at him. Of course, what she saw was not a monster but a breathtakingly beautiful young god. She was so startled that she spilled oil on his shoulder and woke him up. And Cupid, betrayed, flew away." Gwen wondered about the look in his eyes as he had awakened—shocked, reproachful, hurt? A lot like the look in Scott Stewart's eyes when he had opened that paper?

Tim was silent for a moment. "What happened to her?" he wanted to know.

"All sorts of terrible things." Gwen sighed.

"And him?"

"He went home to Mother to recover from his burn."

"How did it end?"

Gwen frowned a little. "I don't remember."

Tim grinned easily. "Sounds like it would make a hell of a movie." But, inside, his thoughts were much more intricate and confused. Gwen, a woman of unequaled variety and never-ending surprises, hidden depths and unfathomed currents—she could outshoot any man on the force and outswear most of them, and then she could sit through an entire hockey game thinking about an ancient love story. He had seen her drag an abusive husband off in cuffs, with a countenance that could kill, and then later had found her packing a basket of "a few neccessities" for the wife and children. There wasn't a cooler head to be found in a crisis, but she could blow up quicker than a twenty-year-old radiator at a balky coffee machine or a slow county clerk. He had seen her drag bodies out of the tangle of metal and smoking asphalt without blinking an eye, and he had seen her kneeling in the street over a puppy hit by a car, with tears streaming down her face. As soft as a rose petal, as hard as tempered steel—sometimes she scared him. All the time she fascinated him.

Tim could not remember the time when Gwen had not been a pivotal part of his life. He had never been quite certain why he could not tell her so. It might have had something to do with the awkwardness of making a pass at a woman you had known since she had braces and scabby knees—or who had known you since the same time. It might have been simply that he knew, somewhere deep on an unexamined level, that Gwendolyn Blackshire—delicate breezes and foamy tides, rainbows and lightning flashes—could never belong to him.

"Cupid, huh?" he said now, his musing tone disguising a deeper emotion. "Hearts and flowers and little cherubs flitting around with a sackful of arrows... kind of strange thoughts for Deputy Sheriff G. Blackshire, don't you think? What brought all that up?"

Gwen lifted her shoulders, stretching her legs out and propping them on the coffee table. "I don't know. Thinking about false impressions, I guess. Psyche chose to believe the obvious, and poor Cupid ended up being betrayed in his sleep because of it. He didn't mean to deceive her and she didn't mean to betray him, but they both ended up getting hurt, anyway. That's life, I guess."

"She was only doing what she thought she had to," Tim reminded her, and Gwen sighed.

"Yeah. A lot of dirty deeds come wrapped in good intentions." Then she smiled, straightening up. "I'm beat. How about turning off the tube so I can hit the sack?"

Tim wanted to draw her head back on his shoulder and coax her to tell him what was really on her mind. And then he was afraid to find out. He wanted to turn her in his arms and kiss her and hold her and tell her that, whatever it was, he understood. He wanted to hold her all night.

But what he did was rise easily and cross the room to take blankets and a pillow from the closet, tossing them to her. And all he said was, flinging a cheerful grin to her over his shoulder as he crossed to his own room, "You're taking me out for breakfast in the morning, kid. You've eaten me out of house and home."

But the bubble of laughter in her voice made his spine tingle, and a warm smile spread through him as she called back, "Good night, Mr. Scrooge. Sleep tight."

"HEAVY DATE TONIGHT, huh?" teased Annalee as Gwen rushed to get out of the office the next afternoon.

"Right," retorted Gwen, pulling on her coat. "With my washing machine."

"Sounds kinky to me," conceded an evening-shift officer in passing, and Gwen ignored him.

Last night she had made up her mind. Who was this Scott Stewart character, anyway, to make her

a fugitive from her own home? She was going to
live in her little cottage on the beach, and he was
going to live three miles down the road for a good
part of the foreseeable future, and she had no intention of regulating the rest of her life around
avoiding him. She must have been temporarily in-
sane even to allow it to get this far. Besides, it had
been three days. If Scott Stewart hadn't come
storming up to her door in a blind rage by now,
he wasn't likely to, and so what if he did? But he
wouldn't. Did Gwen, for one minute, think he
made a habit of pursuing every woman who had
ever served him a subpoena or begged his signa-
ture on a petition or waited on his table in a restaurant, for that matter? It was ridiculous. He
probably hadn't wasted a single thought on the
whole episode, and it was high time Gwen got on
with her own life.

"No kidding," she continued to Annalee, flinging her purse over her shoulder. "I've got two
weeks of laundry piled up. I just haven't been
home much lately."

"So I noticed," murmured Annalee. "Oh,
well, I guess that's what lovers' spats are for. A
girl has to do her laundry sometime."

"Oh, for goodness' sake, Annie," exclaimed
Gwen in exasperation. "You already have us having lovers' spats and we haven't even—"

"Aha!" chortled Annalee triumphantly. "So
there is someone!"

"You're impossible!" groaned Gwen.

"Happy laundry," called Annalee, and Gwen
closed the door behind her.

She had gotten out early for a change, and the

late March sun was still well up in the sky. Soon it would be time for hibachi steaks and sunbathing on the beach, and Gwen wondered how Scott Stewart would spend the summer.

The same way he did last summer, Gwen reprimanded herself firmly. *Without you.*

The only thing that amazed Gwen now was that it had taken her almost three full days to get over a single brief encounter that had not, even to the wildest imagination, included the remotest hint of intimacy. She had finally stopped daydreaming about receiving an "all points" over the unit radio, to report to the house on Beachwood Lane to break up a wild party or check out a burglar alarm or something equally dramatic, of striding into Scott's home in full uniform, hand on weapon, stance militant, ready to do battle with the enemies of the law. She had stopped imagining herself jogging innocently down the beach one fine spring morning and bumping into another jogger who just happened to wear the astonished face of Scott Stewart. She had stopped remembering how sweet he looked while he slept, with his hair tousled and his arm thrown over his head, and how strong and lean his thighs were. Three days. She hardly thought about him anymore at all.

Gwen did not stop for dinner on the way home. She had not been in before ten any night that week, and she had a lot of housework to catch up on besides laundry. Because of the manpower shortage, her next day off was over a week away, and she simply couldn't let it all pile up until then. She had cabinets filled with junk food and sandwich makings, and she would snack through the night between loads of laundry and vacuuming and cleaning her oven.

What she really would have liked to do was make herself a tall drink and lounge on the deck in the balmy afternoon air, watching the sun go down over the Pacific. But discipline was a virtue with which Gwen was intimately acquainted, and she resolutely pushed the temptation aside. Immediately upon entering the house she changed into a comfortable gray flannel warm-up suit with pink stripes down the sides, tied her hair up in an old scarf, and went around the house opening windows. She had sprinkled the carpets with soil remover, started the first load of laundry, and was sorting the second by the time the six-o'clock news came on. She did not know why she was surprised when the door bell rang just as she was spraying the oven with the nasty-smelling cleaner. That stuff had to be timed perfectly, and it never failed that if she got involved with an intricate job, someone always came to the door or called on the telephone.

She should not have been surprised, either, when she stripped off one messy elbow-length rubber glove and opened the door. After all, she had been expecting it all week.

"Hello, Wendy," said Scott Stewart politely. "It's nice to see you again."

Chapter Seven

Gwendolyn stared at him. He was wearing cocoa corduroy pants that molded themselves to his taut pelvis and lean thighs the way corduroy was never meant to do; stovepipe pant legs covered the ankles of shiny brown boots. His white velour sweater had brown piping around the collar and down the sleeves; it was unzipped to midchest. Gwen could see the straining of breast muscles and the dip of sternum she remembered so well, the smooth, delicate brown color of his skin. The wind had tangled a few strands of his hair, but otherwise he appeared freshly groomed, and she caught the hint of a tangy after-shave. He was wearing rimless wraparound sunglasses with amber-tinted shades of the type preferred by motorcyclists and parachutists, and he looked cool, stylish and unruffled. He looked as though he had just stepped off the pages of *Esquire*, and he intimidated her. *So this is what he looks like in clothes,* she found herself thinking incoherently, and then he spoke.

"May I come in?" Scott inquired, still very politely.

"I...I'm cleaning my oven," Gwen blurted ungracefully, but she backed away from the door just as though he had issued a decree instead of a request.

"I won't get in your way," Scott promised, and he stepped inside.

Irritated by her sudden attack of flustered awkwardness, Gwen turned and strode back to the kitchen. *Naturally,* she thought. *Naturally, he would show up when she was dressed in a baggy sweat suit, with her hair tied up in a scarf and oven goo all over her elbow-length rubber gloves.* What was he doing here, anyway? Was he angry? She couldn't tell. She should offer him a drink or something. One did not invite a man into a kitchen to watch one clean the oven; it tended to make a bad impression.

"Watch the fumes," she advised over her shoulder as Scott followed her into the kitchen.

Scott glanced around the room and decided. "I'll sit over here."

An inner groan wrenched Gwen as he made his way across the room to the kitchen table. The door was open to the alcove that hid her washer and dryer, and the washer was merrily chugging away. Forming sloppy piles all across the room from alcove to doorway was two weeks' worth of dirty laundry. Scott edged between the laundry and the table and pulled out a chair—out of her way, as he had promised, but then he was distracted by a pair of lavender panties, caught by the leg opening, on the back of the chair.

He hooked his finger under the garment and lifted it delicately off the chair, examining it for a moment with what Gwen considered unwarranted interest. She took a hasty step to snatch it from him, and he cocked an eyebrow at her endearingly. "You show me yours and I'll show you mine?" he suggested.

Gwen barely caught a giggle as he let the panties fall into the appropriate pile, and for a moment she just looked at him, her lips tight with bubbling laughter, her eyes dancing. All day long she had been trying to tell herself that she had forgotten what was so attractive about him. She hadn't forgotten.

He lowered himself into the spindly chair, stretching his legs under the table, leaning back with his hands folded on his chest. Oh, yes, that same spark of something adorable about him was still there, but today there was something more. The last time she had seen him he had been a confused little boy with all the charms and frustrations associated with such. Today he was a mature man, calm and in control, exuding a subtle aura of virility as he lounged at her table in his amber sunglasses and his sweater unzipped to his chest. Still charming, still easygoing, still sexy as hell. But grown-up.

For some reason, that made Gwen uneasy.

"Coffee?" she offered brightly, and he shook his head. Suddenly unable to think of anything else to say, Gwen turned back to her oven. She could feel him watching her steadily through his amber-tinted glasses.

Sunglasses, she thought cynically, holding her breath as she opened the oven door. A gust of acid air greeted her. He probably had had another one of those rough nights. Although why that should concern her she did not know, except that he still hadn't explained why he was there, and if he was drunk or stoned, she wanted to know about it before the conversation went any further. She pulled on her glove and scraped a pile of charcoal into the trash can with a battered sponge. The washing machine spun to a stop.

"Do you want me to put the clothes in the dryer for you?" Scott volunteered.

Gwen cast him a startled look. Startled that he offered, or startled that he actually knew where clothes went after they left the washing machine? She wouldn't have thought Scott Stewart ever had to worry about performing such chores for himself. "No, thanks," she replied, dragging more leftover casserole-and-roast drippings and the overflow of apple pies into the trash can. "I'll get it." She gave him another quick glance before concentrating her attention on the interior of the oven again. "I don't imagine you came over here just to do my laundry."

There. It was out in the open, and in his court now. Gwen rinsed out the sponge and waited for his reply.

She could almost hear the rueful smile in Scott's voice. "No, I guess I didn't."

She turned to face him. Still, he was watching her steadily behind the protection of his glasses. "Then why?" she inquired simply.

Gwen could see nothing of his expression except the vague curve of his lips. It could have been bitter, sarcastic, shy or expectant. Dammit, why didn't he take off those glasses? How was she supposed to communicate with a man who hid his eyes? Scott said, a little hesitantly, she thought, "It took me these past three days to make up my mind to come over here."

"Why so long?" she inquired with every pretense of lack of interest. Of course, she knew the answer.

He lifted one shoulder negligently. "I had a lot of stupid thoughts. I guess I was angry at first. I felt betrayed, for some absurd reason. I felt like a fool—which, no doubt, I was—and I didn't want to compound the error by making a big deal out of it to you."

"And now?" Gwen kept her voice very even.

"Now I'm curious, for one thing," he replied easily. "I'd like to hear the whole story."

Gwen swallowed hard. She had nothing to be ashamed of. Why did this suddenly seem so difficult? She firmly pushed her silly reservations aside and faced him squarely. "I'm a deputy with the sheriff's department. Part of my job is to serve subpoenas."

"Deputy?" he inquired with interest. "How about that? I've never known a deputy before. Must be quite a job."

He sounded sincere, but Gwen could not be sure, and she refused to let it rattle her. She couldn't be sure of anything when she could only see half his face. "So, anyway," she started to continue with a breath, but then she just couldn't stand it anymore. "What in the world are you hiding behind those glasses?" she demanded irritably. "Another hangover? Drug fatigue? A black eye?"

He looked surprised and then confused; then he reached up and pushed the glasses away. "Sorry, officer," he apologized blandly. "They're photosensitive," he explained. "Sometimes I forget I'm wearing them." His eyes were sea-green, clear, and just as beautiful as she remembered them. They watched her openly and patiently as he pushed the glasses up over his forehead to rest casually in his hair. The effect was very sexy. "Go ahead," he invited.

Once again Gwen was flustered, and once again she tried not to show it. Damn him, anyway. Was he never predictable? She tilted her head in what she hoped was a casual gesture. "That's about it. When I came to your house, you were obviously in no condition to accept a legal document, and then I was afraid you were going to kill yourself running around in the dark and—" she shrugged "—things got out of hand from there."

The slow, relaxed smile that lightened his features was entirely unexpected. "That's good," he said quietly, with stated relief. "I really couldn't believe you were one of those sharks who would go to any lengths to get her man." And he quirked an amused eyebrow. "So to speak."

"So to speak," murmured Gwen wryly. She stripped off her filthy gloves and dropped them in the sink, then turned to look at him hesitantly. "You're not mad?"

He shrugged. "Why should I be?"

Now Gwen was beginning to wish he had left the glasses on. His eyes were entirely too bright, too knowing, much too compelling. He did not miss a nuance with those eyes. She felt compelled to be out of range of his gaze, and she crossed behind him to transfer the clothes to the dryer. "Most people have an inexplicable dislike for process servers," she told him dryly, bending over the washing machine. "I can't imagine why."

"Oh, that." His voice dismissed it. "Stuff like that doesn't bother me. I was just a little bit offended when I thought you might be doing it all as some sort of elaborate game." There was a half question in his voice, but Gwen did not turn to meet it. "But sometimes you have to go with first impressions. And my first impression of you was that you were very sincere. I think you meant everything you did and said that night."

Gwen turned to him, her arms full of stiff, damp laundry, now on guard. "I didn't do anything that night," she reminded him distinctly.

But he only smiled. "Sure you did. You cared about me, Wendy," he said so guilelessly that it went straight to Gwen's heart. "I don't know if anyone has ever done that before for me—freely, without ulterior motives, and it meant a lot." He saw an uncomfortable protest forming, and he went on smoothly, "You cared enough not to let me drown or fall down the cliff and break my back. You took me home and sobered me up, and you didn't have to do any of that. You talked to me like a real person and," he added with a short, dry laugh, "you wouldn't believe what a change that is." And then he grew serious again. "I didn't want to believe any of that was just pretense, and it wasn't. I'm glad."

What could Gwen say to that? He made it sound so simple, sitting there with his racy sunglasses and his sexy sweater and his devastatingly clear eyes. He made it sound as though that one evening spent together had been important to him, too, but what did she know about this man? She had wanted to see him again—she had wanted quite desperately to see him again. Well, here he was, and Gwen did not know what to do with him. She turned to dump the clothes into the dryer.

"Well," she declared a little nervously, "I'm glad we got that straightened out." She turned on the dryer and then turned back to him, trying to look easy and relaxed and...dismissing. "It's nice to know you're not the kind of person who holds a grudge, and thanks for coming by to tell me so...."

Her voice trailed off, and Scott just sat there, watching her unwaveringly. The man certainly was big on eye contact. "I did say," he reminded her in a moment, "that I would see you again."

"Yes, well..." She gave a quick little smile and flipped her hair behind her ear. Scott's eyes followed the movement.

"See you again," he elaborated meaningfully, "as in the generally accepted context of the phrase, 'seeing you,' as in all those quaint little social things a man and a woman do when they're trying to get to know each other, seeing a lot of each other."

He delivered it all so deadpan that Gwen had to laugh. "I knew what you meant," she admitted, a dimple forming in her cheek. But then the practical side of her nature took over and she had to add, however reluctantly, "And that's all very nice, Scott, but—I mean, you're not exactly drunk and helpless now, and surely you can see . . ."

She let the words trail off, hoping he would get the meaning, but he chose to be obtuse. "See what?"

She sighed. "A person doesn't just decide to be interested—" was that the phrase she was looking for? Oh, the archaic difficulties of language! "—in another person because of one meeting under really bizarre circumstances. I'm glad you're not mad at me, and it was . . . interesting . . . meeting you, but—" again she released her frustration in a breath "—we really don't have anything in common, and I don't think there's much promise in seeing each other, as you put it."

He lifted on eyebrow, undisturbed, his eyes never wavering. "No? What don't we have in common?"

"Oh, for goodness' sake." Her voice held a note of exasperation. "Look at you, with your half-million-dollar house on the cliffs."

"Is that what it cost?" he interrupted musingly. "I never knew."

"That's exactly what I mean!" Gwen replied, exasperated. "You and your wild celebrity parties and your built-in pool," she continued intrepidly, "and your international companies and your flocks of women and—well, everything! I'm not interested in any of that stuff, and you certainly aren't interested in my kind of life, so—" she shrugged, spreading her hands "—what else can I say? It seems pretty obvious to me."

Scott studied her thoughtfully, but a lurking spark of amusement in his eyes confused Gwen.

"You must have given this a lot of thought," he observed, and she frowned. "You also," he pointed out when she moved to avoid his positively nerve-stripping gaze, "have a terrible tendency to make snap judgements; you should work on that. Celebrity parties and international companies? Now who's confusing me with my brother?" A note of something very close to disappointment came into his voice then, and it embarrassed Gwen. Then he let it go, and the little hint of amusement in his eyes grew to something definite and quite appealing. "As for the flocks of women," he confessed modestly, "well, I'm afraid there aren't any. You see, I have a real problem with self-confidence. It turns most women off."

Gwen looked at him skeptically. "And I'll be delivering a mortal blow to your ego structure if I turn you down, right?"

He smiled. "Well put."

What he lacked in self-confidence, he more than made up for in intimidation techniques, Gwen observed dryly. First arouse the maternal instinct, then appeal to the decency of human nature, then cast the responsibility of his whole self-image on the object of his intent. Very clever. Very clever, indeed. Of course, Gwen would never fall for it ... unless she wanted to.

Gwen turned to adjust the washing machine and poured a measure of detergent into the dispenser. Why was she making it so hard on herself? What difference did it make whether they had anything in common or not? They weren't getting married, for goodness' sake! Gwen usually wasn't so picky about the details of the men she chose to date—or chose for friends, she amended to herself quickly. There was no reason to be so judgmental about Scott. He was attractive, interesting, and maybe she even liked him a little. She had already had this debate with herself. Why did she suddenly feel the need to be protective of emotions?

Out of the corner of her eye she saw Scott reach into the low pocket of his sweater and draw something out, which he unobtrusively slipped into his mouth. *A pill,* Gwen thought. *That's why,* she told herself grimly. What do you know about this man? You should have stuck to your first impression.

But she also should have known by now to expect the unexpected from him, for the last thing Scott Stewart would be was stereotyped. He must have caught her suspicious glance because he blandly drew out the package from his pocket and held it up to her. "Cough drops, officer," he said mildly. "Want one?"

An attack of mirth twitched at Gwen's lips, prompted both by something uncannily resembling relief and by the memory of the last time she had seen him, strolling down the beach in the March wind. Snap judgments indeed. "Have a cold, do you?" she inquired with a very poor imitation of sympathy. She had to turn away to hide the dancing laughter in her eyes. Ah, the wages of sin.

"Raging sore throat," he admitted, tucking the package back into his pocket. "Which only means—" she turned just then to scoop up another load of laundry, and caught the light gleam of speculative sensuality in his eyes, the easy softening of his voice "—that I can't kiss you now, either. More's the pity."

Gwen stopped midbend, and she straightened up slowly, looking at him with a curious, lazy smile. She was unaware that, to Scott, that smile was almost more of an invitation than he was able to refuse. Gwen was not trying to be alluring or provocative; she was just thinking. All things considered, he had been fairly understanding, more so than she had expected. He had come back here; he wanted to see her despite a bad start. And Gwen supposed that, despite all her logic and common sense and very natural reservations, she was glad he had.

She shook her head a little. "You're a very strange person," she murmured.

Scott lifted both eyebrows dramatically. "Because I want to kiss you?"

She laughed, turning back to the washing machine. "Because of a lot of things."

"Good or bad?" he persisted.

Gwen pursed her lips, still facing away from him. "Both, I think," she decided, and set the water temperature.

"Well," he conceded with a lift of his shoulder, "that's a start. Does that mean I can take you to dinner?"

She turned back to him. Well, this was what she had been waiting for, wasn't it? In all those barely repressed daydreams of the past few days, wasn't this always a part of what she had envisioned? Romantic candlelight dinners, soft glances across the table, hours of conversation, some earnest, some laughing . . . getting to know each other, delighting in each other, having fun together. It was so easy to imagine; why did it suddenly make her so nervous? Touching, caressing, and finally . . .

She swallowed hard, looking quickly around. "I've got all this laundry to do and—" she glanced dubiously down at her flannel-clad body "—I'm a mess, and—"

"Quick dinner," he promised. "Home before ten. And very informal. You don't even have to change. Come on." He smiled persuasively, a little mischievously. "A free meal is a free meal, right?"

Gwen looked at him, one corner of her lips turning down wryly. "It didn't take you long to discover my weakness."

His eyes sparked as he tapped his temple knowingly. "Amazing powers of perception," he assured her. "Shall we leave now, or do you need to wash something to wear tomorrow?"

"No, all my uniforms are clean." She swept the scarf off her head and hesitated for a minute. "Are you sure you don't want me to change?"

"No problem," he said gallantly, rising. "It's going to be a very casual evening."

A man couldn't be all bad, reflected Gwen as he put his hand lightly on her back and they left the house, if he could, without blinking an eye, take a woman out for a first date who was wearing a sloppy sweat suit and dirty tennis shoes. Maybe they had more in common than Gwen had first imagined.

But when they walked out into the late-lingering haze of sunshine and Gwen saw the gleaming midnight-blue Porsche, she began to reconsider her opinion. "Nice car," she murmured, sidling up to it.

Scott glanced at her before lowering his sunglasses. "Good tires, excellent gas mileage and only driven back and forth to church on Sundays."

"Looks like it should have teeth," commented Gwen, observing with cautious respect the ferocious scowl the front fender formed between the headlights.

Scott grinned and opened the door for her. "Relax. It hasn't bitten anybody yet."

For some unknown reason Gwen remembered that his mother had been afraid to get into Rick's Cadillac for fear of soiling the seats, and that made her smile. Besides, Scott looked so happy and relaxed that it was hard not to share his mood.

"I know a great taco stand just up the highway," Gwen volunteered as he put the car in gear.

Scott made a face, backing the car into the street with a careful efficiency that somehow was at odds with his racy sports-car-driver image. "Tacos," he said. "Can't stand them."

"Oh-oh," Gwen mumbled. "I think our relationship has just hit a major stumbling block."

Scott grinned at her. "After what our relationship has survived so far, I think we can handle it."

And Gwen realized suddenly that the word "relationship" sounded good when applied to them. It was easy to say.

Maybe that was why she had been making it so hard on herself.

Scott did not get a chance to show off the speed of the slick sports model on the winding streets they were taking, and in fact, he drove with a caution and an ease of command that surprised Gwen. She would have thought reckless-ness was in his nature, and very little told as much about a man as the way he drove a car. Not averse to high-speed traveling herself, Gwen nonetheless enjoyed the ride along the cliffs overlooking the coast, with the sun in her face and the wind tangling her hair. At points where the view was clear, the ocean below looked like a sheet of tinted cellophane that was ruffled by the wind; the dark contrast of brown beach and black rocks was almost too perfect to be real. Gulls hovered and dived toward the shiny silver glow of the sun, and here and there along the roadside colorful crocuses and wildflowers were beginning to poke through. Gwen never got tired of look-ing at this part of the world.

So absorbed was she in the view that she did not notice immediately where they were going. When she did take note, she thought Scott might be doing no more than taking the long route to the highway. It wasn't until he swung the low-slung car into the incline of his own driveway that Gwen cast him a narrow look. "My, we do move fast, don't we?"

"I promised you casual," he returned cheer-fully, and switched off the ignition. He bounded out of the car and Gwen followed more reluc-tantly.

"Don't look so suspicious," he challenged her righteously, meeting her in front of the car. "We have—" he glanced at his watch "—three hours and fifteen minutes before I have to take you home, and it makes a lot more sense to me to spend it talking and relaxing than fighting the crowds at a restaurant. Besides—" he shrugged "—I don't like to go out much."

"Um-mm." Gwen shot him a guarded look from beneath her lashes. "Bet you say that to all the girls."

He touched her arm to lead her up the steps. "Not to worry." He grinned. "Fortunately for you, our relationship has not progressed to the stage of intimacy where communicable diseases are something we share. I'm sick, remember?"

"Right," Gwen returned, but her voice was still heavy with mock sarcasm.

He did not lock his door, Gwen could not help noticing as he gestured her inside. Somehow that seemed typical of him. The law enforcement officer within her was offended; the woman who had put his seminude form to bed only three nights ago was not surprised.

"Do you want something to drink?" he offered, crossing the room. His voice echoed a little off the teak floors and vaulted ceiling. "I think there might be some wine left over from the party."

"Sure," Gwen agreed absently. "Sounds nice." But she was mostly absorbed in taking full advantage of the first opportunity she had had to study the house of Rick Stewart's brother.

The room was nice, but nothing about it was particularly extraordinary. Three steps from the foyer led down to a sunken living room decorated in pale earth tones. The walls were white, with framed geometric prints—not prints, Gwen corrected herself mentally, but undoubtedly originals—in bright oranges and reds and yellows. The pit group was beige, the occasional tables were glass, the fireplace was white brick. There was an enormous schefflera in one corner that grew from floor to fifteen-foot ceiling. An open dividing wall led down three more steps to the dining room, on the table of which Scott had been dancing the first time Gwen had seen him. No rugs marred the gleaming beauty of the floor, and a picture window with plain beige draperies looked out over the rock garden. There was a small semicircular bar opposite the fireplace, and it was there that Gwen followed Scott now.

He had found a bottle of white wine in the refrigerator under the bar, and he applied the corkscrew deftly. There were cut-glass decanters on the bar, but all of them were presently empty. "Here you go." He filled a wineglass and passed it to her.

Gwen took a sip and raised her eyebrows appreciatively. "Good."

"Is it? It's imported, I think." Scott opened the small refrigerator again and took out a Diet Coke for himself.

Gwen couldn't help smiling as she watched him pour the soft drink over a glassful of ice cubes. "You really don't drink?" Her voice was a little high with amusement.

"Really." He lifted his glass to her. "A toast." His brow wrinkled with thought until he decided, "To the next three hours."

Gwen's eyes twinkled as she touched his glass with her own. "Here's to hoping you can cook."

And Scott's eyes danced back at her. "Here's to hoping you won't be too mad when you find out I can't."

Gwen widened her eyes in mock outrage and he choked back laughter. "No, no, I promise I'll feed you." He flung up a hand defensively, then took a quick sip of his Coke. "As a matter of fact, I'll make it the first priority. Have a seat, relax—I'll be back in a minute."

He set down his glass and started toward the dining room, and Gwen called after him, "Do you mind if I look around the house?"

He stopped and for a moment looked puzzled; then he shrugged. "Help yourself."

It was uncouth, she knew, but Gwen couldn't resist the impulse to see how the other half lived. Besides, she rationalized defensively, he had seen every part of her house; it was only fair. And Annalee would be wanting a full report.

Actually, it was not too much different from anything she would have expected to find in *Better Homes and Gardens*. From the living room another short set of steps led upward to a short corridor, off which two rooms opened. One was a bedroom, as clean and as bland as any hotel room in the country; the other was a good-sized bathroom with an aqua motif and soaring sea gulls on the wallpaper. At the end of the corridor were two more steps that led downward into the largest bedroom Gwen had ever seen. The walls were glossy navy-blue, the carpet white, the furnishings Danish. Gwen held a general dislike for the low, efficient lines of Danish decor, but she had to admit that, in this house, for this man, it fitted. Sleek, attractive, bold. A king-sized bed covered in a white coverlet, with graduating dark-blue squares etched upon it, dominated the room, accompanied by an equally huge dresser. Scattered through the room were low sling chairs, a glass table or two, a writing desk and a couple of thick loungers, one in white with blue piping, one in blue with white piping. A set of glass doors led to the wraparound deck that looked over the ocean. A wall unit opposite the bed held artistically spaced books, objets d'art and a portable television set. On one shelf was a small pottery vase that whimsically held a dyed-to-match navy-blue carnation; on another shelf was a ceramic piggy bank. Other than that, nothing about this room suggested that the man who occupied it had any personality at all.

She wandered into the adjoining bathroom, and her eyes widened with appreciation. In size it easily equaled her own bedroom at home. The fixtures were a deep-maroon color; the tile was pale sandstone. The countertops picked up the navy blue of the adjoining room, and the effect was incredibly stunning. A skylight poured in overhead sun, and a collection of healthy green plants that lined the steps to the round sunken tub thrived in it. There were double vanities and one mirrored wall. There was a separate shower enclosure and a sunlamp alcove. Gwen's feet sank into the plush navy carpeting. Like the bedroom before it, it was unmistakably a man's room, but here she discovered, to her very great

delight, were the signs of life that had been missing before now.

One plush maroon towel hanging on the rack
was rumpled and damp; another one was crum-
pled carelessly on the vanity. There was a smear of
toothpaste in the sink and soapy fingerprints on
the faucet. Shaving cream was uncapped, razor lying on the edge of the sink, blow dryer on the
vanity with its cord trailing to the floor. There
were damp footprints on the carpet beneath hers
and beads of moisture on the shower door. A pair
of jeans had been carelessly discarded in the
corner. Apparently he had showered and changed
just before he came to see her, and the familiar
tangy odor that filled the room came from the
after-shave he had spilled on the countertop.
Somehow the entire effect pleased her, and Gwen
left the room smiling secretly to herself.

It wasn't until she met Scott in the living room
again that Gwen realized what was missing from
the tour.

"So," Scott queried cheerfully, taking up his
glass from the bar again, "did you thoroughly analyze my personality by examining the way I decorate my home?"

Gwen cocked an eyebrow thoughtfully. "Pretty
much."

"And?"

"Cool, reserved, emotionless," she decided.
"A little compulsive. Emphatic, logical, always in
control."

"Ha!" His eyes danced with laughter. "Got
you this time. I didn't decorate it," he told her,
winking as he passed by her toward the dining

room again. "It was done before I ever moved in."

Gwen shrugged, following him. "A minor technicality."

"Leaping to conclusions again," he reprimanded her over his shoulder. "You've simply got to learn that things aren't always as they appear to be."

Gwen sipped her wine, giving the dining area a cursory glance. It was relatively small—apparently he did not give too many sit-down dinners—dominated by the inlaid-wood pattern on the dining table and the six leather-and-chrome chairs that surrounded it. There was a closed buffet on one wall and the glass doors through which Gwen had followed Scott outside the last time she was there. Three more steps led down to a roomy copper-and-stainless-steel kitchen. It was, like everything else, immaculate.

"Who's your housekeeper?" she inquired.

He gave her a brief, amused glance. "I am. I told you, I don't like having extraneous people around. Besides, I like doing it; puts a real challenge into the day."

A quirk of her lips indicated what Gwen thought of that statement. "That explains it, then," she observed sagely.

He glanced at her as he took a head of lettuce from the copper-tone refrigerator. "Explains what?"

"Why your housekeeper didn't get around to cleaning your bathroom yet."

For a moment he looked a little disconcerted; then he gave a regretful little shake of his head.

"How careless of me. Accept my apologies, please. I just wasn't expecting any visitors in my bedroom tonight."

Wasn't he? The little twinkle in his eye as he placed the lettuce on the chopping block caused a funny crawling sensation in Gwen's stomach, and she took another sip of her wine. "What's for dinner?"

He nodded toward the open door leading onto the deck, where a grill smoked fragrantly. "Hamburgers." And he lifted a warning eyebrow. "Otherwise known as tacos without the hot sauce."

She grinned. "And here I had my mouth all set for pâté de foise gras and pheasant under glass."

"We could send out," he suggested, and Gwen laughed. She was having a good time. She hadn't fully expected to, but she was. And Scott looked as though he had anticipated it all along.

Scott turned over the making of the salad to her while he formed fat hamburger patties out of a concoction of meat, eggs, soy sauce and dehydrated herbs. "My own secret recipe," he informed her, and they worked companionably for a while. Then Gwen had to broach the question that had been bothering her since she entered the house. "Scott," she inquired curiously, "why aren't there any pictures or mementos of Rick around the house? I expected the walls to be full of them."

The small upcurve of one corner of his lips seemed a little vague. "Yeah, I guess you did." He placed the last patty on the platter and wiped his hands on a towel. "I don't have any," he said simply. "Everything goes into the museum—or museums. Nothing of Rick's is privately owned, except, of course, by the collectors who were lucky enough to get their hands on some souvenirs before he died."

Gwen puzzled over that, and she felt a small twinge of a poignant tug at her stomach. What must it be like to be unable to keep for himself even a small reminder of the brother he had loved—to know that the world had first claim on all that was left of Rick Stewart? Death must be so much more final when there was not even a memory you could call your own.

Scott took up the platter as Gwen scattered the last of the chopped mushrooms over the salad. "Bring your drink," he invited. "Let's sit out on the deck and watch the sun set."

"So," Gwen said, settling into a comfortable canvas chair with her wine. "What do you do besides throw wild parties and cook hamburgers?"

Scott carefully slid the hamburgers, one by one, onto the sizzling grill. The aroma of butane-heated coals, hickory chips and smoking grease was pungent and delicious. "Not much," he answered, then flashed a quick, amused glance at her. "Oh-oh. I see I've offended your Puritan work ethic again."

"You've got to do something," Gwen responded, a little more irritably than she had intended. He read her too well. "You manage Rick's estate, don't you? All those companies, the museums, the charities?"

"Not really," he replied without interest, carefully closing the cover on the grill. "The lawyers do most of that." He went back into the kitchen, continuing through the open door, "Lyle—you might have met him at the party the other night—he's sort of like my liaison. All the big shots decide what needs to be done, Lyle tells me about it, and I sign the papers." He returned through the door with his glass of Coke in hand. "And that's all there is to it."

A disturbed frown shadowed Gwen's face. Though she resented his "Puritan work ethic" reference, Gwen did find something slightly offensive about his role in the whole thing. It smacked of the lazy rich-kid syndrome, and never one to keep her opinions to herself, she said, "Sounds awfully inefficient to me. They could be robbing you blind."

Scott laughed. "Not likely. Everything connected with Rick Stewart is subject to such public scrutiny that it has to be squeaky clean—even now."

"It doesn't bother you to just sit back and let somebody else run it all?" she insisted. "I mean, don't you feel any sense of responsibility?"

An uneasy shadow crossed those steady green eyes, but he was still smiling. "It wouldn't matter if it did. You're talking to a guy with a major in art history and a minor in dead languages—what do I know about running a business?"

"So what did you know about being head of a security team?" Gwen challenged.

"I saw every Kung-Fu movie ever made," he returned spiritedly, took a sip from his glass and shrugged. "I don't know. I just always knew I'd end up working for Rick, and that's where he needed me most."

Very strange, thought Gwen, but she decided to let it drop for now.

But Scott noticed her disturbance. It showed in his eyes, which never once flickered from her, and in the brief, awkward silence that followed. Then he said brightly, "Tell me about being a deputy. How did you get into that line of work? What is it you do, exactly? Do you wear a gun?"

Gwen laughed, a little nervously, Scott thought, and she turned her eyes to her wineglass. "It's not as exciting as television might make it out, I'm afraid. Mostly routine stuff."

"No headin' 'em off at the pass, no eleventh-hour rescues, no dramatic courtroom scenes?" Scott teased.

Gwen shook her head, then drained her wineglass. The setting sun bounced off her hair in coppery rays when she did that. "Nothing so overwritten," she assured him. "Mostly writing tickets and giving lectures at the elementary schools and—" her eyes twinkled "—serving subpoenas."

Scott met her glance with a grin and reached for her wineglass. "Strange are the ways of fate," he murmured provocatively. "Just think, if you had had a real criminal to chase you might never have met me."

He went into the house before she could retort.

Scott returned with a fresh glass of wine for her and with his own glass refilled, and he sank down into the deck chair opposite her. "Tell me all about Gwendolyn Blackshire," he invited expansively. "Every dull, boring and excruciating detail."

She laughed and made that attractive little motion of flipping her hair behind her ear. "That should fill about three minutes."

"No, really," he insisted, leaning forward a little, with his elbows on his knees. "How did you get into police work?"

"Oh, I don't know." Her eyes wandered toward the orange-and-lavender sunset; her voice was casual. "Too much television when I was a kid, I guess. In law enforcement everything is black and white. I like that."

He smiled a little, grasping that little insight into her personality as though it were solid gold. "Nice," he agreed, "as long as everything stays black and white, and as long as you can be sure you can tell the difference."

Gwen looked at him. "What do you mean by that?"

He made a small dismissing motion with his shoulder and took a sip of his Coke. "Things aren't always that simple," he pointed out. And a mischievous twinkle crept into his eyes. "Take me, for instance. That first night we met, you had me pegged, didn't you? Turns out I'm nothing like the wild-and-crazy rich playboy you thought I was."

Gwen laughed, and sparks of sun caught in her eyes. "You're not, huh?"

"Not a bit," Scott assured her, fascinated by the prisms of light dancing in her eyes. "First of all, I'm not rich. The house, the car—" he glanced around deprecatingly "—they come with the territory. Money-wise—" he shrugged and took another sip of his drink "—I probably don't have much more than you do. Fortunately, they pay me much more than I'm worth. As for being a playboy—" he pulled a regretful face "—I never learned how, I'm afraid. Despite his reputation, Rick led a very clean life, and he was twice as strict with his brother as he was with himself."

"That still leaves 'wild' and 'crazy,'" Gwen pointed out.

His eyes sparkled endearingly. "That," he allowed generously, "you can judge for yourself."

"Better not," Gwen demurred. "I have a tendency to make snap judgments. Besides," she added, sipping her wine. "A very wise man once told me the only thing that it's ever important to see clearly is what is inside ourselves. When you understand that, everything else falls into place."

"Can you do that?" Scott asked curiously. The soft absorption with which he studied her seemed to perceive her answer before she gave it. "Can you see yourself that clearly?"

Gwen had to lower her eyes. His gaze, at times, became a little hard to take. "Sometimes," she answered. Her voice sounded softer than she meant it to be. She looked at him again. "Most of the time."

He nodded, as though he understood completely. "I guess," he acknowledged, "that has to be a pretty important ability for a law officer. Knowing exactly what you can do, how you will react in any given situation, trusting yourself, I suppose, always to do the right thing." He seemed to muse over that for a moment. His uncanny perception both amazed and intimidated Gwen. "Funny," he said. "I guess most of us never have to think about ourselves that much. Know ourselves that well. We might be better off if we did." Then he looked at her. "Seems like awfully dangerous work to me. Doesn't it ever scare you?"

Gwen took another sip of her wine, avoiding his eyes. Sometimes he understood entirely too much. Besides, she didn't like to talk about her work, especially to strangers. "Not really."

Scott started to pursue the subject, but something in her expression dissuaded him. He got up to turn the hamburgers. "Have you always lived around here, Wendy?"

"Um. Most of my life. Those smell good."

"They are," he assured her. "You're in for the gastronomical treat of your life." He resumed his seat and took up his Coke again. "Do you have family living near?" he wanted to know.

Gwen shook her head. "My father died a few years back. I inherited the cottage from him." She was aware, not for the first time, of a very disturbing trait of his. He always looked one straight in the eyes, never wavering, never flinching, almost fixedly. It was not an intimidating gaze, merely an interested one, and it was a very unusual characteristic. He hardly seemed to blink. It made Gwen feel stripped.

"Your mother?" he inquired casually.

"She left when I was six," Gwen replied. She didn't mean to sound short, but she did. She wished he wouldn't look at her like that. As though there was nothing he didn't see. "I'm really starving, you know," she said, a little bit too enthusiastically. "How much longer?"

He glanced at his watch. "Three minutes till rare. Do you want to bring some candles and eat out here?"

"Sure." Gwen set her wine on the deck beneath her chair. "I'll help."

They brought dishes and candles, hamburger buns and salad and a huge package of chips out to the patio table, and feasted in the blue twilight and the ocean breeze. True to his word, Scott's hamburgers were superb—or it might have had something to do with the night air or the flickering candlelight ... or maybe even the company. In the soft shadows of the candlelight, Gwen didn't even mind Scott's staring at her so much anymore.

"Have you ever been married, Wendy?" Scott asked unexpectedly, relaxing in his chair. He had eaten half his hamburger and a few bites of salad, then had foregone the rest of the meal in favor of his soft drink and another cough drop. Gwen felt a twinge of amused sympathy for the condition of his throat, but it did not in any way impair her own enthusiastic enjoyment of the meal.

She laughed, startled. "Good heavens, no. What brought that up?"

"I told you," he explained patiently, "I want to know everything about you." And there was a peculiar spark in his eye. "Even if I have to drag it out of you one word at a time."

Something uncomfortable warmed Gwen's neck under the cover of night that felt suspiciously like a flush. It was probably just the candles. She dismissed it negligently and crunched a potato chip.

"I guess I'm just not used to being interviewed," she admitted. "Pretty much a private person, like you." She deftly turned the tables on him.

He lifted an eyebrow. "Me? I've got no secrets."

"Neither have I," she retorted, and then, before he could ask her to prove it, she pursued, "You said you moved out here for the isolation, and that you don't like having people around. Why is that?"

He thought about it for a minute. "The isolation," he decided, "was because, I suppose, I spent so much time in such a hectic life-style that a house on a deserted cliffside began to sound like heaven to me. A deserted island would probably have been even better." Simple enough, thought Gwen. She could accept that. "As far as not liking people," he continued, "I didn't mean that exactly. I'm just particular about my company. That probably comes from so many years of protecting Rick from the crowds. It gets to be second nature."

Again, perfectly reasonable. He had all the answers, nothing to hide, nothing to evade. "So what about the party?" she wanted to know. "How did all those people end up in the same place at the same time?"

"It wasn't exactly my idea," he admitted ruefully. "Most of them live in L.A. or San Francisco—except for Lyle, who just lives over in Sausalito—and I don't see them very often. When they decided they wanted to give me a birthday party, I couldn't exactly refuse, could I?"

Gwen looked at him meaningfully. "You could have refused that first drink."

He lifted an eyebrow, eyes dancing in the dark. "Touché."

The breeze tossed the candle flames around like twin tennis balls, creating a cacophony of color and shadow on the table, on the dishes, on Scott's face and in his eyes. The ephemeral glow of orange and gold across the planes of his cheeks and tangled in the strands of his hair was unearthly and enchanting, making him look more like something she had dreamed up than a flesh-and-blood man. The sound of the ocean below was mesmerizing, the night itself a gentle aphrodisiac, and it was easy to imagine . . .

But that was foolish, Gwen reprimanded herself sternly. Hadn't she just spent a good portion of the evening telling Scott about the value of being able to see people clearly? Fantasizing did nothing but cloud the judgment, and there was no room for it in Gwen's life.

"Ex-husbands, boyfriends, children," Scott said suddenly, easily, "tell me about them all."

Gwen gave a nervous little sound of startled laughter. "None of the above apply to me," she assured him. "What's for dessert?"

His eyes widened in mock insult. "What? The pleasure of my company isn't enough for you? You still want more?"

More, Gwen thought unexpectedly, her eyes wandering without volition to the lean, strong lines of his throat, to the soft curve of his lips. *Oh, yes.* She swallowed on a suddenly dry throat and reached for her nearly empty wineglass. She had the most uncanny feeling that he had seen right through her and caught that fleeting and highly irrational thought, because when next her eyes brushed across his, there seemed to be a softening there, a spark of something vital. She said, feigning disappointment, "Well, in that case, I may as well help you do the dishes."

"You're only required to help with the dishes after a full-course meal," Scott replied, rising, "and since I so thoughtlessly failed to provide dessert..." He began to clear away the plates. "You sit here and relax. Do you want some more wine?"

"No, thanks." She emptied the glass and handed it to him with a wink. "I know my limit."

Scott grinned and disappeared into the kitchen.

When he returned, Gwen was standing against the rail, looking out over the ocean. The wind ruffled her hair and occasionally snatched at her clothing, for a moment outlining the shape of her hips or her waist. The sharp profile of her jaw was tilted upward as she focused her vision on the dark horizon in an almost aggressive, but nonetheless alluring, way. In the dim flicker of the candlelight he could see the graceful shape of her hand as it rested on the rail, soft and white. She had very small hands, he noticed for the first time; the shape was square, with short, compact fingers, strong yet graceful. He wanted to feel those fingers against his skin. He wanted to touch her hair, to rearrange the strands the wind had tangled, to feel the texture, thick and glossy, against his palms. He wanted to tuck her hair behind her ear as she did and feel the warmth that nestled between neck and scalp. He wanted to inhale her fragrance. He wanted to touch her, and the wanting made his throat dry.

Scott came toward her noiselessly. He stood beside her for a moment and only a slight movement of her muscles acknowledged his presence. "Heavy dreams?" he inquired softly.

"Um." She smiled quietly and lifted her face to catch another drift of cool sea air. "I'll bet you spend a lot of time out here, looking at the ocean, dreaming your life away."

"It's pretty hard to resist," he admitted. Gwen felt his fingers very lightly grasp an errant strand of her hair and smooth it gently into place. The gesture caused a prickling sensation on the back of her neck. She could feel him close to her, the wild cherry scent of his breath faint and sweet, his warmth something tangible. She did not turn to look at him, but she did not want to move away.

"What do you dream about, Scott?" she asked softly.

A woman like you, he wanted to answer. He let his hand trail down—oh, so very lightly—to the place her hair curled against her neck. Gently, he stroked the bare flesh there. A smile crept into his voice. "I don't know. Captains and kings, I guess. Being young again, growing old...all sorts of things."

The gentle caress of his fingers against her neck was working a peculiar arrhythmia in her chest. She tried to ignore it with the lightness in her voice. "No magnificent obsessions, no grand ambitions? You don't want to save the world or run for president or build an empire?"

He chuckled. "Not me." One hand rested on her shoulder; the other came up and lightly cupped her other shoulder. He just held her like that, no part of him touching her but his hands, loosely and gently. But his touch seemed as intimate as an embrace, and Gwen felt something slowly melting within her from the warmth of his hands. "Sometimes," he said simply, very quietly, "I dream of nothing more than moments like this."

Gwen felt everything within her tense, yet her muscles remained pliant and relaxed beneath his hands. That was the time, she knew, when he should have made a move. He should have bent and kissed her or turned her into an embrace, and her pulse quickened in anticipation. But he did nothing. He simply made a statement—sweet, unadorned, honest—and he was content to do nothing more than touch her. She was both confused and strangely moved. Who was this man with the unwavering, all-seeing crystal eyes, the gentle smile, the perfect body? Scott Stewart—unpretentious, easygoing, open and unashamed. Unambitious, unconcerned, irresponsible. Scott Stewart, the coal miner's son, heir to an international kingdom whose existence he barely acknowledged. Rick Stewart's little brother.

She turned around slowly; he dropped his hands. She looked at him gravely. "What do you want with me, Scott?" she asked simply.

If he was disconcerted by the frankness of the question, he did not show it. He brought his hands up and gently tucked her hair behind both ears, his palms lingering lightly against her face. And he looked at her seriously.

What did he want from her? Everything. And nothing. He wanted to tell her that on a windy night she had walked with him on the beach, picked him up when he was down, protected him from himself, made him look at things he hadn't wanted to see. He had felt something start to change within him that night, to shift gradually into focus. She talked to him as though she expected more of him and had made him, briefly, expect more of himself. She had asked him questions he couldn't answer. She was still doing that.

He wanted to tell her that she was the most special thing that had ever happened to him—that she stood out against the gray backdrop of the rest of his life like a yellow diamond. He wanted to tell her that he had fallen asleep in her bed with visions of mermaids and angels dancing in his head and that he had awaked in love. It would sound stupid to tell her that. It sounded stupid even to think it.

He said simply, "More." His voice was quiet, a little hoarse. "I want more of you. To see you, to touch you." His fingers trailed down, outlining her throat, an uncertain smile shadowing his lips. "To know you. To be a part of your life, somehow. Do you think that's possible, Wendy?"

Gwen met the steadiness of his eyes, the trace of anxiety lingering there, for as long as she could. What place was there in her life for him? Was he strong, dependable, steadfast? Was he simple and solid like her father, unpredictable and reckless like some of the men on the force? Was he the gentle, lonely man he claimed to be, or was he the flashy rich kid she had first imagined him to be? All of the people in Gwen's life fitted into neat little categories. Scott Stewart was a potpourri of everything she did not understand; nothing about him could be categorized or labeled.

"I don't know, Scott," she said at last, softly, and she moved away.

Scott let his fingers trail down her arm and she half turned from him, and the movement left a lingering path of warmth. She was sorry when he was no longer touching her. He turned to lean on the rail, looking at the ocean and not at her. Gwen wondered what he was thinking. She wondered, if she could see his face now, whether there would be hurt there or disappointment. She suddenly hoped not. She did not want to do anything to cause him hurt. As the silence grew she began to worry. Was this it, then? Would he take her answer as a refusal or a show of lack of interest, and would he give up on her? Would she never see him again? That possibility disturbed her immensely.

And then, slowly, he began to chuckle. Gwen turned sharply, a mixture of relief, confusion and irrational concern tightening her voice. "What are you laughing about?"

He had been looking down at the cliffside and the beach below; now he glanced at her, amusement mixed with a shy ruefulness still sparking in his eyes. "I was just thinking about how we met," he confessed. "Couldn't have been under worse circumstances, could it?"

A series of scenes from that night flashed through Gwen's mind, and her own lips tightened with repressed giggles. "You do make a rather bad first impression," she agreed.

"Well, then." His voice softened, and so did

his eyes, as he touched her arm. "I'll just have to work twice as hard to overcome it, won't I?" And without giving her a chance to reply, he smiled and exerted a mild reassuring pressure on her elbow. "Come on. I'll take you home."

Chapter Eight

There was nothing uncomfortable about the silence during the five-minute drive back to Gwen's house. The night air blowing through her hair was chill and invigorating, and it made her wish that the Porsche did not have bucket seats. She wondered if Scott would have put his arm around her while he drove, and if she would have snuggled up to him for warmth. She tried not to wonder why he had actually kept his word about taking her home early. She hadn't really expected him to.

"What was that subpoena for, anyway?" she asked curiously in a moment. She knew it was unprofessional to display such a morbid interest, and that it was really none of her concern, but she wanted to know, anyway. After all, it had brought them together.

The lights from another cliffside mansion floated by, then a stretch of tangled shrubbery. Scott glanced at her. "I don't know," he answered without much interest. "I just turned it over to Lyle."

Gwen stared at him, unable to hide the astonishment in her eyes or her tone. "You're summoned for a court appearance, and you don't even know what for?"

Scott shrugged and slipped another cough drop into his mouth. "Some lawsuit or another, I suppose. Besides, it's not really me they want, it's Ricky's estate."

"But—" Gwen's voice was hesitant with incredulity "—don't you even care?"

"Things like this happen all the time," he answered. "Most of it I don't know anything about and wouldn't understand if I did."

Still Gwen shook her head, not comprehending. She turned to watch the slow-moving scenery in blurred colors of dark blue and gray-green and told herself it was none of her business. But it was incredible. Wasn't he even curious? "It could be important," she insisted, unable to keep silent any longer. "This time it could be something you knew something about."

Again he shrugged. "Lyle will tell me if it's something I should know. Can't imagine what that would be, though," he added thoughtfully.

"But don't you even want to know?" she demanded. "How can you not want to know? Your name was on that paper; it's your brother's estate—and when it comes right down to it, isn't it your money? It just seems to me you'd want to know," she finished, somewhat disgruntedly, and settled back into the seat.

Scott slowed the car as they approached her driveway, and he took the opportunity to look at her—to examine her, so it seemed. "Would you like me better," he asked in a moment, pulling the car to a stop in front of her house, "if I did know?"

Gwen had no trouble returning his gaze this time, long and steady and reflective. "I think," she admitted at last, "I might like you better if you took things more seriously. If you were more responsible."

Scott looked at her, and he felt a strange, gentle yielding inside him. Pretty Wendy, so unlike her name, an officer of the law who was responsible for the lives and welfare of everyone in the county—she knew when to take things seriously. What did she want from him? He was not what she saw in him, but neither was he what she wished him to be. In thirty-one years he had never felt a need to change anything about himself—he went where circumstances dictated; he let others direct and he followed easily; he had never asked for control or power and it had never been offered to him. Why should anything change now? Why should he change?

He shook his head briefly, a small smile lifting the corner of his lips. "That's what makes the world go round, Wendy," he said. "I'm me and you're you. We each handle things differently, I suppose. Maybe," he suggested, "you could learn to like me in spite of my faults?"

Or maybe even because of them, Gwen thought, and his smile was so persuasive that she couldn't help returning it, however reluctantly.

They got out of the car, and he held her hand as they went up the walk. It was a natural gesture, easy and unconstrained, and it reminded her of the last time he had held her hand, on the beach.

Had it only been three days ago? What a large part of her thoughts he had occupied since then.

Gwen unlocked the door and turned to him. "It was nice tonight, Scott." She smiled and meant it. "Great hamburgers, terrific atmosphere, stimulating conversation. Thanks."

"I can make steaks, too," he volunteered, and grinned. "After that, my menu starts to go downhill, I'm afraid."

Gwen laughed. "After your throat gets better, I'll have to introduce you to the joys of a really well-made taco. It's the jalapeños that make the difference," she confided.

He made a face, but there was a lingering spark of something soft and deep in his eyes at her invitation. "I'll do my best to look forward to it," he said.

She smiled again, a little uncertainly, and started to say good night. But he captured her hand again and lifted it slowly, dropping his eyes to study her palm. The expression on his face in the moon-induced shadows was vague and tender, and it somehow made Gwen's pulse jump. He brought his other hand up and traced a light, tingling pattern on her palm with his forefinger. It was warm and stimulating and vaguely erotic. Her breath caught as he brought her hand gently to his lips and kissed the place where his finger had touched.

The gesture was heartbreakingly sweet, yet unexpectedly sensuous. His lips were soft, just as soft as Gwen had imagined them to be, and the warmth of his breath left an imprint on her skin. Then she felt the tingling, stimulating moisture of his tongue skipping delicately over the pattern of her palm, and little sparks of electricity danced along her skin.

Her fingers curled as his tongue moved with infinite slowness away from the sensitive center of her palm and toward her wrist. She could feel the light, tripping motion of her heart, and she was breathing faster. Gwen had never imagined a sensation like this. The tip of his tongue was smooth and abrasive, delicate yet powerful. The flower-petal flesh beneath the moist, heated trail he blazed was fired with nerve endings, shooting erratic, potent impulses to other parts of her body—to her throat, which grew tight, and to her stomach, which registered a tingling, drawing sensation, to her breasts, which seemed to fill with new awareness. Slow movements, lazy and warm, tingling all the way up her arm and spreading outward, pinpointed now on the lightly veined skin that covered her skipping pulse in a deep, erotic, circular pattern. How easy it was to imagine his lips, his tongue, working their magic on other parts of her body. How would they feel on her neck, her ear, her breasts, her mouth, drawing deeply and hungrily? How would it feel to thrust her fingers into his hair and capture the taste of his lips for herself, to feel his lean, strong body enfolding hers? Her knees actually weakened, and she lifted her hand to his arm for support. All of this from no more than the touch of his mouth upon her wrist.

Slowly, he lifted his face. The moisture left on her skin grew cool with the night breeze, but the rest of her body was very warm. She could feel the stain of anticipation on her cheeks, and her fingertips still tingled. "Next time," he smiled, and brought her hand once again upward for a brief final kiss, "I won't be contagious." The smile deepened, and he looked at her for a moment longer. His eyes were starlight-bright. "Good night, Wendy," he said softly.

Gwen did not remember whether or not she returned his good night. She hoped so. Because she found herself looking forward with unexpected pleasure to the next time they met.

Scott, who never slept well at night, found going to bed an impossible notion after leaving Gwen. He wandered around the big house for a while; he watched television; he got up restlessly and began to pace again. He tried to settle down to read. He put on one of Rick's old records. His mind kept going back to the time spent with her. Every moment, every word, every look and gesture—he examined them over and over again, and each time he found some new delight, a deeper yearning.

She was reluctant, uncertain. Probably he should be, too. She was cautious; he was impulsive. She was pragmatic; he was carefree. Perhaps they would balance each other out. Or perhaps she would never give them a chance. She had every reason to be wary of him, he had to admit. They had gotten off to a bad start. And the worst part was that so much of what she thought about him had its basis in truth. She was beginning to see things within him that Scott himself had never realized or bothered himself about. And maybe she was right.

At about twelve-thirty he wandered into the

bedroom; he started to undress. The room seemed so empty, the bed so large. He smiled a little, reluctantly. That bed would never look comfortable to him again until she was in it.

He sat down beside the telephone and spent another thoughtful moment staring at it. Then he lifted the receiver and punched out a number.

The grumpy, sleepy-sounding voice on the other end of the line did not affect him. This, after all, was what the man was being paid for. "Lyle," he said curtly. "Do you remember the subpoena I gave you the other day? Open it up and read it to me, will you?"

Scott tolerated the growls and complaints and liberal expletives until the voice on the other end of the line came fully awake and was able to direct a coherent question to him.

And Scott hesitated for only a moment. The answer sounded strange, even to him. "Because I want to know, that's all," he said, and settled back to listen.

Chapter Nine

Matt Breckenridge, sheriff of Paos County for the past seven years, cleared his throat absently and pushed aside a few papers on his desk to make room for his coffee cup. It was a subtle sound, but enough to bring the collection of officers that crowded into his small office to immediate attention. Matt was like that himself—small and wirily built, with a soft voice and deceptively mild blue eyes. There was nothing about his physical appearance to command awe. But he ruled with an iron hand; he knew when to be harsh and when to be tolerant, and his officers were as dedicated to the man as they were to the job. He commanded a tight and efficient team, one of the best in the northern part of the state.

He said now, taking a sip of coffee while he glanced over a notice on his desk that had just caught his attention, "I guess you're all wondering what's up, and I'll get to that in a minute. First, though—" he pushed the paper aside and absently adjusted his wire-rimmed glasses on his nose "—I'd like to have a word with you about interdepartmental misconduct. Deputy Blackshire—"

the sheriff fixed her with a piercing gaze "—you
have got," he said distinctly, "to learn to control
your temper and stop beating up on my duty officers. It's a waste of taxpayers' money and very
bad for morale."

Grins and good-natured nudges went around
the room, and Gwen had the grace to look
abashed. Still, she knew Matt was only half joking,
and that the reprimand was intended for the officers who harassed her as much as it was for
Gwen herself. She was glad when the focus
moved off her and on to the real purpose of the
two-shift meeting.

"All right." Matt leaned back in his chair, his
expression serious, his gaze direct. "What I called
you all together for was this. Looks like trouble is
heading our way, and we've got to be prepared for
it. Seems like there's a drug ring operating somewhere within the Denim-Lasser-Monroe triangle,
and the state boys want our help on it. Chances
are, we won't even have to get involved, but I've
promised our cooperation and we have to be
ready for anything. Let me tell you what I know
about the situation as it stands."

Gwen listened alertly, took diligent notes, mem-
orized the photos of possible suspects. Her training had been excellent; she knew exactly what her
role would be in any one of the possible scenarios
the sheriff projected. Her mind was working with
clear, efficient accuracy, and she did not miss a
detail. And inside, a cold fist had started to close
around her stomach that was gradually spreading
its paralyzing chill to her spine.

Big cases were rare in the Paos County sheriff's department. There was an occasional prison break or hostage situation—before Gwen joined the force there had been a mass murder and one shoot-out that had cost two officers their lives—but large-scale drama was the exception rather than the rule. Chances were, as Matt said, that they wouldn't even get involved, but he would not have been briefing them if the possibility did not exist. And it was that possibility that terrified Gwen.

Every day was dangerous, of course. The routine could flare into unexpected violence at any time, and Gwen never forgot that. But in her two years on the force Gwen had never faced an armed robber, never apprehended a felon, never surprised a perpetrator in the act of a crime. She had never had to draw her weapon. Wondering what she would do in a real life-and-death situation was what gave Gwen nightmares at night, and that was what she could not talk about with anyone. Not even Tim.

"Sound tough, don't they?" Tim commented to her as they left the office to start on patrol.

"Drug pushers usually are" was her only comment.

Tim had been a San Diego police officer before he joined the Paos County force. He had faced his test and passed it many times. If he knew what fear was like, he didn't show it. And he would have been the last to suspect that Gwen Blackshire, one of the sharpest, most efficient officers on the force and the most courageous woman he had ever known, broke out in a cold sweat every time the radio crackled a crime report.

Tim shrugged. "We'll probably never get a crack at them, more's the pity. I'd like to teach those guys a lesson. We don't stand for that kind of crap in this part of the state."

Gwen regarded him in amused tolerance as they stepped out in the morning sun. "Tim, you're so damn macho you make me want to throw up sometimes."

He grinned and tossed her a lazy salute as he climbed into his unit. "Catch you at lunch, babe."

"I am not a babe!" she called after him, knowing full well he used the term just to annoy her. He acknowledged her with another grin as he drove off.

Both she and Tim were on highway patrol today—long, lonely jobs that nobody on the force liked. There was danger in being only one man to a car, a fact generally acknowledged and little talked about, one of life's little unpleasantnesses forced upon them by economics. When they were on desk duty they took assignments in pairs, but that was only when they were being sent to the known scene of a crime. Gwen usually did not think about the danger too much when she was on the road alone; it was the tedium that got to her. But today she thought about the danger.

She thought about what Scott had said to her last night. "Things aren't always black and white." Everything within Gwen that made a good law officer rebelled at that. That was the trouble with the criminal justice system today, too much blurring of the lines, too much shading of the truth. And that was the advantage of being on this end of the system. There were no judgments to make, only duties to do. Let the lawyers and the D.A.'s and the judges screw it up after the fact; Gwen's job ended when she made the arrest.

But it was the lingering knowledge that things might not always be that simple that disturbed Gwen. She had not needed Scott Stewart to put it into words for her; Gwen had always known it. And what if, at the crucial moment, she could not make the right judgment? What if, when it mattered most, the difference between black and white was no longer clear?

What if she froze?

Scott had wanted to know how she had gotten into law enforcement. His question had made Gwen uncomfortable because it reminded her of only one more thing she didn't know about herself. She supposed, if she had to analyze it, that it probably had a lot to do with trying to prove something to herself...and to her father. Still among her most precious memories was the look of pride in her father's eyes whenever she presented him with a new accomplishment. "You're so unlike your mother," he used to say, and his eyes would mist over with a mixture of sorrow and pride. "Not that your mother wasn't a good woman." He had always made a point of finding something complimentary to say to Gwen about her mother. "But deep inside, she was a quitter, Wendy. She just didn't have what it takes to go the distance. There was something weak inside her that gradually gnawed away all the fine qualities she once had." And then he would smile.

"But you're not like that, Wendy. You're solid gold through and through."

So Gwen continued to achieve, continued to present her father with honor rolls and sports awards and leading roles in school plays. Gwen was always steady and honorable and upright, independent and self-sufficient and responsible. Law enforcement was a logical step for her. Her father had been very proud. And Gwen had never stopped wondering whether, deep inside, she might have inherited whatever weakness it was that had caused her mother to walk out on a loving husband and a six-year-old child. Gwen still wondered whether she had what it took to go the distance.

And that small kernel of self-doubt, which she consistently tried to abolish and generally managed to ignore, was exactly what made her so uneasy when trying to deal with the phenomenon of Scott Stewart on a logical basis. She didn't like the way he haunted her. She didn't like the pull he seemed to have on her whenever she was with him. It was very, very hard to trust her instincts on this one—mostly because she did not entirely know what her instincts were.

During that long and mostly uneventful day Gwen found her mind repeatedly returning to Scott. She had better things to worry about, it was true. She had to keep her mind on her job and it was becoming increasingly hard to do. Once already this week Scott Stewart had preoccupied her thoughts to the point where she had let her guard down, and the resulting injury to Mickey could have been serious. Next time might catch her in a real crisis, with real lives depending on her ability to think straight and think fast. She did not have room for this in her life.

And the solution to that? *Stop fighting it, Wendy. Relax and enjoy it.* Gwen smiled a little at that, because it sounded exactly like something Scott would say.

Gwen had not had many close personal relationships with men in her life, and those she had indulged in had been singularly short-lived. She thought she understood the reasons for that. Most men found themselves intimidated by a woman who excelled in what, perhaps more than any other profession in the world, was still considered to be an unquestionably male job. Of course, she reflected, Scott had not seemed to be too concerned with that. And Gwen knew that she wasn't the easiest person in the world to get along with; she was too direct, too outspoken and blunt for the taste of those who liked to play those flirtatious courtship games. Not that Scott had seemed to object to that characteristic, either; seeing as how he was unquestionably one of the most open men she had ever met, how could he? But there was another, deeper reason for Gwen's comparative lack of success in the department of romance, and she frowned a little as she admitted it to herself. Commitments were easy when everything was lined up in black and white. People, as Scott had so astutely pointed out, were rarely that uncomplicated. Gwen did not like to be wrong. It whispered and nagged at her that her first-sight impression of Scott Stewart had been slightly off base. What if she was now only seeing

what he wanted her to see? She had judged him
rather harshly the first time, and it was now beginning to appear that she had been wrong. What if
all the warm and pleasant things she had seen in
him last night were only a product of more mis-
judgment on her part, and what if she did not find
out until it was too late? It was a valid concern.
Gwen's risk-taking capabilities were confined to
her job; in her personal life she preferred a much
simpler existence.

She sighed, knowing that the best thing for her
to do was simply to forget Scott Stewart and all the
complications he brought into her life...and
knowing she was not about to do any such thing.
If only he could have been a little less complex, a
little easier to understand—more predictable,
more stable, more consistent. Like Tim, she
thought. Now, there was a man who was exactly
what he appeared to be: simple, steadfast, single-
purposed. No hidden depths or secret currents.
You always knew where you stood with Tim.
Then Gwen smiled to herself and shook her head
a little, knowing full well that Scott Stewart was
none of those things, nor was he likely ever to
be—and that was exactly what fascinated her
about him.

It was after ten when Gwen got home that
night. Any other time, she might have considered
staying in town, but tonight—she admitted it
shamelessly to herself—she wanted to be home in
case Scott called. And sure enough, just as she put
her key into the lock, the phone started to ring.

Of course, the key got stuck. She was carrying a

bag of groceries, and it ripped the minute she stepped over the threshold, spilling spaghetti and oranges and half a bag of candy all over the living-room floor. Cursing the bag boy and fumbling for the light switch, Gwen crushed most of the spaghetti under her heel as she rushed for the phone. It must have rung ten times by then. She answered it breathlessly, just when she was certain the party on the other end must have hung up.

"Where the hell have you been?" an irate male voice demanded of her. "Do you have any idea how long I've been calling you?"

Gwen did not know whether to be outraged or amused by the possessive demand in his voice. In the end, a smile won out, and she was surprised that how she actually felt was warm and cared for. It was not an altogether unpleasant sensation. "Now, how would I know a thing like that?" she returned, relaxing into a deep rattan chair and slipping off her shoes. "I wasn't here, remember?"

"Well, where were you?" Scott was too agitated to take the reprimand or notice the teasing in her voice. "Didn't you know I'd be worried?"

Gwen started to retort that she had no way of knowing that he would even call, but such touching concern on his part made that kind of reply sound callous, even to Gwen's ears. Of course he was worried. He did not know her well enough to be otherwise. "Sometimes I have to work late," she explained, not impatiently. "I would have been home on time tonight, but I took in a prisoner—"

"A prisoner?" he interrupted sharply. "Was he dangerous?"

Gwen couldn't help grinning when she tried to imagine eighty-year-old Willie Cox, whose only great vice was a love affair with a bottle of rum, as dangerous. He had been spotted weaving down the center lane of the highway—on foot—just as Gwen was preparing to take her unit in. Naturally, she had picked him up. "Only to himself," Gwen assured Scott. "But I had to stay and do the paperwork. Then there was a fender-bender on Highway 12." Why was she explaining herself to him? Perhaps because it felt good to have someone to explain herself to. "No injuries, but time-consuming." She combed out her hair with her fingers and drew her feet beneath her, relaxing in the chair. That warm feeling that had first struck her when she heard the sound of his voice was beginning to spread all over her body. It felt good. "So," she invited, "what have you been up to today?"

His laugh sounded a little self-conscious. "Nothing, compared to what you have. I'm sorry I yelled at you when you answered the phone. It's just that I expected you to be home about five, and I thought something might have happened to you." Gwen was struck by how easily he made a confession that would have embarrassed another man, how he could show such concern for a woman he barely knew. That touched her.

"I'm hardly ever home by five," she told him, smiling. "Those are the things you have to get used to when you're involved with a law officer."

Had she really said that? Had she said "involved"? What was she doing, putting words in his mouth?

But Scott did not seem to notice the slip, or if he did, he did not find anything unusual about it. He chuckled easily. "Yeah, I guess so. I won't be so paranoid next time. I was hoping we could have dinner tonight," he added.

"How about tomorrow night?" she suggested, and immediately was stricken with a wave of uncertainty. The word "involved" kept echoing in her head. Was she really sure she wanted to get involved with him?

But he answered, "I can't tomorrow night. I have a meeting with Lyle. How about Sunday? We could have a picnic or go sailing or whatever you want. Spend the whole day together."

"I have to work," Gwen said, and the stab of regret she felt was genuine. A whole day with him sounded marvelous.

"On Sunday?" he objected.

Gwen's smile was rueful. "Who do you think is keeping the world safe for democracy while the rest of America is reading the comic strips and sunbathing on the beach and watching the ball game on television?"

His voice was wry. "It's a dirty job, but somebody has to do it, right?"

"Right." It was so good to talk to him.

"Well, okay, then, Sunday night. Can you get home by eight? I'll take you someplace nice."

Gwen lowered her eyebrows dubiously. "On Sunday night, around here? I doubt it. We'd have to drive all the way to Sausalito, and by then it would be too late to eat. Why don't you come over here and I'll cook?"

She could hear the low laughter in his voice. "I thought you'd never ask."

"Con artist!" she returned, wrinkling her nose. But her eyes were sparkling and her skin was tingling. She could almost see the tousled hair and cellophane-bright eyes from here. She wondered what he was doing as he talked to her. Was he lying in bed, pillows stacked behind his head, torso bare, blankets arranged loosely low on his abdomen? Was one lean arm stretched over his head, tightening the muscles there, while his other hand cradled the phone against his cheek? Was he smiling as he spoke into the receiver?

It was late, she reasoned. He could be in bed.

"How's your throat?" she asked. She half intended it to be merely a polite question, but of course it came out as much more than that. And she wasn't entirely sorry.

There was a short silence. Then Scott answered softly, "Much better." The implied promise in the statement actually made her fingertips tingle, and that embarrassed her.

She said quickly—and rather stupidly, it seemed to her later—"I still have laundry to do." Of course, she would much rather talk to him. What did it matter if the piles of dirty clothes that were still scattered all over her kitchen floor started to grow mold? If a telephone conversation with him was all she had, she wanted to prolong it for as long as possible. Who cared about laundry at a time like this?

His laughter was low and delightful. "Okay, I'll let you get to it, then. I'll see you Sunday." Gwen had the sudden and most absurd impulse to invite him over, right then. Forget the telephone, forget waiting until Sunday and forget, most assuredly, the laundry. Forget it was after ten and she had to be up at five-thirty in the morning. She just wanted to see him.

And then his voice gentled a fraction, and he said simply. "I missed you today, Wendy."

Gwen's eyes closed slowly. I missed you, too. "Good night, Scott," she said softly.

"Good night, love."

Gwen replaced the receiver as though it were a sacred object.

HE APPEARED ON HER DOORSTEP at five minutes before eight on Sunday evening. Gwen had been home since six, shampooing her hair, polishing her nails, deciding on exactly which one of her extravagantly feminine hostess outfits to wear. When she opened the door, a dish of Polynesian chicken was simmering in the oven, tender asparagus tips were waiting for the hollandaise sauce and Hawaiian bread from the warming rack wafted its sweet scent throughout the house. She was wearing an ankle-length, fully pleated skirt in sheerest cotton, festive in its delicate blue-and-pink print, but just casual enough for the occasion. The shade of her blouse exactly matched the bright pink hue of her nails, and its airy sleeves contrasted modestly with the daring dip of the ruffled neckline. Her lips were glossed a pale rose, and the brightness of her eyes hardly needed the enhancement of smoky-blue shadow. She felt vibrant and feminine, which was its own reward, but if she needed further gratification, it was abundantly present in Scott's eyes when he saw her.

His shirt was a pale peach-orange color, open-throated, turned up at the cuffs to reveal strong-boned wrists. His slacks were dark charcoal, form-fitted and perfect. There was something very sexy about his shirt. The delicate color seemed to reflect on his skin like a flush of anticipation that crept straight to his eyes. Those eyes were clear and as dark as a shady summer lawn; they widened and deepened with pleasure when he looked at her. "Hello," he said softly. He swept her with a glance up and down. "You've changed."

"Ha!" Gwen kept just the right note of mocking reprimand in her voice, but her eyes were dancing, and there was a wonderful airy feeling in her chest. "Bet you thought I never wore anything but baggy jogging suits and old tennis shoes, right? That's what you get for making snap judgments."

He grinned and drew from behind his back a bottle of wine. "Am I forgiven if I brought you a present?"

Gwen accepted the bottle and he stepped inside. She gasped as she looked at the label. "Châteauneuf-du-Pape—" She swallowed back the rest of her astonishment. Obviously, Scott would have no idea of the monetary value of the gift he had brought her. "It's.very nice," she said inadequately.

"It wasn't doing any good sitting around my place," he answered guilelessly and wandered into the living room. Everything about this place looked so familiar to him, so warm and inviting. "Something smells delicious."

"Have a seat," Gwen murmured, still marveling over the wine label. "I'll just check on dinner."

She returned in a moment with a glass of wine for herself, mineral water garnished with lime for Scott. He was sitting on the sofa, his arm stretched across its back, one shiny-booted foot resting on his knee. He looked comfortable and perfectly at home in the airy blue-and-lavender room, and for a moment Gwen just had to stand there, watching him. She could not recall any other man ever looking so right on her sofa.

She smiled and handed him his glass, taking the chair across from him so that she could watch him while they talked. He glanced at his glass curiously. "What's this?"

"Perrier," she returned. "Imbibed in all the best places by all the best people."

"Mm." He took a cautious sip. "Not bad. I've never had it before."

She lifted an eyebrow. "What do you drink at parties, then?" And she grinned. "When you're not falling off the wagon, that is."

He returned her grin with just the right touch of bashful chagrin. "I usually drink Coke," he confessed.

"Not with my Polynesian chicken, you don't!" she retorted indignantly, and he laughed.

"So, Wendy." His voice was soft, his eyes reached out to touch her. "How've you been?"

"Not bad." What had caused her own voice to take on that husky, sonorous quality? She couldn't seem to make herself look away from him. Just looking at him filled her with—she could not define what. It just filled her. She lowered her eyes to her glass because her gaze was becoming somewhat embarrassingly intense, and she took a sip of her wine. It was exquisite.

Gwen looked back at him, smiling. "How about you?"

No pat answers from him. She should have known that. "I guess I never realized before how bad my own company can be," he answered simply, "until the last couple of days. They were long." Then he sat back, a small flicker of self-doubt crossing his all-too-open eyes. He shouldn't have told her that. She did not want to hear that. A hint of apology was in his brief smile, and he took another sip from his glass.

Long days, thought Gwen. They hadn't been exactly short for her, either. Not when every waking moment and most of her sleeping ones were filled with thoughts of him. Not when every bit of her energy was directed toward unraveling the puzzle that was Scott Stewart but only finding new mysteries with every answer. Never getting tired of the search.

A suggestion of a frown shadowed his features when he looked at her again, as though he were wrestling with a decision and he could not decide how much it bothered him. "I did have some disturbing news yesterday," he said, in a moment.

"Your meeting with Lyle?"

Scott looked surprised that she remembered.

Gwen had not forgotten one word of anything he had ever said to her.

He nodded. His smile was half dry, half uncertain. "You got my curiosity up about that subpoena," he admitted. "I had Lyle check into it." And now his frown was not just a hint; it was definite. "Seems some joker is suing the estate for two and a half million. Claims that Ricky's first three songs—the ones that gave him his name— were stolen. Can you believe that?" His voice rose with incredulity, backed by a small laugh. "Even 'Sometimes,' Ricky's theme. Everybody knows Ricky always wrote his own music. Why would he need to steal songs? It's ridiculous."

Gwen released a low breath. Two and a half million. It sounded like an enormous sum to her; to the estate of Rick Stewart it was probably a mere pittance. "What are you going to do?" she wanted to know.

He shrugged and lifted his glass again. "Lyle will handle it. It just makes me mad, that's all. That there are crazies out there who actually think they can get away with something like that."

Gwen knew she should have kept her mouth shut. She had no right and no qualifications to advise Scott about business affairs. But before she knew it, she was saying, "What if Lyle doesn't handle it the way you want him to? Don't you think you should follow this up for yourself?"

He stared at her blankly for a moment. "I'm not a lawyer," he said. "What can I do?"

Gwen sighed. She should let it drop. Hadn't they had this conversation before? "Oh, Scott, I don't know," she returned impatiently. "Something. It is your business, isn't it? It's your brother's reputation."

He dismissed that with a turn of his hand. "The charge is absurd. Everybody knows how clean Ricky was. The case would be laughed out of court." That was not what she meant, and Scott knew it. A disturbed frown furrowed his brow again. Maybe Lyle was right—he was better off not knowing about these things. No point in getting upset over every weirdo who ever tried to make a quick profit off Rick Stewart's legend— there were, Lyle had assured him, hundreds. Scott did not need the complications. And it did make him angry, this ridiculous charge. It was useless to get angry over things that had no basis in reality, things he could not change, and now Gwen was angry, too. He wished that he had not brought it up.

This time, Gwen kept her mouth occupied with the wine and her eyes lowered. She could feel the sweet warm mood of intimacy dissolving around them. She was not going to aid the process any further; she had said enough. She did not want to argue with Scott, not tonight. And she had no right to judge him, to interfere in his life.

She stood up and forced a smile. "I'd better check dinner. Back in a minute."

The table was already set; the chicken and vegetables were perfect. The ingredients were all prepared for the sauce, and Gwen began to combine them with efficient expertise. She did not want to argue with Scott. She didn't want to dwell upon his less worthy characteristics, and she did not want to be reminded how different they really were in their values and basic approaches to life. That shouldn't matter to her. All that should matter to her was that he was pleasant and easy to get along with, that he made her laugh, that they could share good times, that everything about him stirred the woman in her and excited her senses, that he was fun, good-looking and sexy. It shouldn't get any deeper than that.

It bothered Gwen that her feelings already seemed to be deeper than that.

She understood Scott, or at least she thought she did. What must it have been like for a small boy to be plucked out of a hell of deprivation, death and violence and deposited in a single day in a fairy-tale world of white Cadillacs and mansions? He would have been cautious, insecure, greatly traumatized by his childhood, afraid it would all disappear. And his brother had done everything in his power to assure him that it was real, to make him secure, to compensate for all the years that had gone before. Undoubtedly, Rick Stewart would have overcompensated. He would have made Scott forget the ugliness of his childhood by substituting the cotton-candy world of dreams come true and making Scott believe in them. As an adolescent Scott Stewart had been protected, indulged, pampered. He would never have had to face a harsh reality or make a difficult decision. The wonder was, of course, that Scott hadn't turned out to be a complete mess—a reckless, amoral sociopath with illusions of grandeur. A great deal of credit belonged to Rick and to his mother for the reasonably well-adjusted man Scott had become.

But the trouble now was that Scott had lived so long in that insulated world that he was completely lost, now that his focus was gone. The symbiotic relationship between Scott and his brother had been destructive as well as nurturing. Rick took care of Scott, and when he was old enough to assume his position in the hierarchy of the Rick Stewart empire, Scott took care of Rick—or at least he was allowed to think he did. Now that Rick was gone, Scott could not understand that there were still things that needed taking care of; he was totally unprepared to assume the initiative, now that there was no one to give him orders. And it was a terrible waste of a life.

Scott came up behind her. He moved soundlessly, but Gwen was never unaware of his presence. The very air of the room seemed to change when he came into it. "Two more minutes," she said brightly, stirring the sauce.

Scott said, "You're disappointed in me again, aren't you?"

Gwen hesitated, then looked at him helplessly, "Oh, Scott, that's not the point. It doesn't matter what I think."

"It does," he assured her soberly, "to me. So tell me what you're thinking."

Gwen looked at him for another moment, debating, and then turned back to her sauce. She really didn't want to get into this. "It's just," she said, removing the saucepan from the burner, "well, why do you think Rick left you in charge of his estate?" she demanded of him. Nothing good ever came from keeping her opinion to herself.

She turned to him. "He could have easily set up a trust leaving all the lawyers and professionals in charge—the people who, as you claim, know what they're doing. But he wanted you to make the final decisions. Why do you think he did that?"

Scott did not look too concerned. "That's just the way it's done, that's all," he replied. "I was his only living relative; Rick was very traditional about things like that, and that was just the way he wanted to do it."

Gwen carefully ladled a serving of rice, chicken and a garnish of parsley on each plate. She should let it drop. She knew that. "What do you think Rick wanted for you, Scott?" she asked, keeping her voice casual.

Scott watched her alertly. He wanted to give the right answers, but he knew he probably wouldn't. He wished it didn't matter to her so much who he was or what he did with his life but, contrarily, that very concern of hers was what endeared her to him most. She cared. Nobody else cared, not even Scott himself. That was something very precious, and he wanted to honor it. He was sorry he kept disappointing her. "Rick wanted," he answered carefully, "the best of everything for me. All the advantages he never had. The best education, the best opportunities, the best people helping me, travel, material comfort, security—everything."

Gwen spooned a layer of hollandaise sauce over the asparagus tips; then she looked at him. "Do you think he would be very pleased with what you've done with everything he gave you? Don't you think that by sending you to the best schools, letting you work closely with him, giving you a chance to learn from all the people around you—don't you think he was preparing you for something?''

Scott did not lower his eyes; he never tried to avoid eye contact. But the opaqueness that came over his face was just as effective. He said in a moment, gently, ''That was all in the past. There's nothing I can do for Rick now.''

Still, his whole focus was Rick, what he could do for Rick. There was no room for Scott in his own vision of his life; Scott did nothing for himself. Gwen knew it was cruel, but the words were out even before she was aware of them. ''Rick is dead,'' she said simply. ''You're not. You can't go on living as if you don't exist.''

She saw the brief flash of shock in his eyes, and Gwen knew she had done a terrible thing. It wasn't so much that she had hurt Scott; she had alienated him. Always talking too much, always being too blunt—their relationship wasn't strong enough yet to take that much honesty. Didn't she learn anything from her mistakes? Scott would probably walk out now, their lovely evening would be ruined, and any chance they had ever had to discover what lay between them was ruined forever. She mourned the fact before it even became a reality.

But then, to her very great surprise, Scott smiled. It wasn't much of a smile, to be sure, but it was an effort. An effort to reassure her that he wasn't angry, that he wasn't offended, that he wasn't going to give up on them so easily. He took the plates from her and carried them to the table. "Do you want to know something?" His voice was matter-of-fact, almost casual, as he found her glass and refilled it with wine. "You were right when you said that Rick was still controlling my life. That night of the party there was a lot of guilt and sorrow mixed into the celebration, and it probably had a lot to do with my drinking too much. I had just never thought about it before." He smiled at her, more naturally this time, as she touched a match somewhat nervously to the candles on the table. "You've given me a lot to think about," he said quietly.

Scott held her chair for her, and Gwen's relief that the evening was not irretrievably spoiled was overwhelming. "I talk too much, sometimes," she admitted, wanting to apologize. "You shouldn't let me interfere in your life."

The gentle light in his eyes was all-absorbing. "I want you to interfere in my life," he told her simply, and the quiet statement for some reason sounded like an invitation or a promise. It made the flesh over Gwen's spine tingle. It made her so happy that she felt almost buoyant. "But," he added, and a light sparkle came into his eyes that relaxed them both immediately, "while we eat, do you think we could have some lighter topic of conversation? Like crime, urban blight, the crisis in the Middle East? Do you have any controversial political views or maybe a sensitive religious issue or two we could debate? Anything to aid the digestion."

She laughed and picked up her fork, her eyes twinkling. "Let me think about it," she suggested, and she loved the way his face seemed to catch the light of the candles when he smiled.

Throughout dinner—which Scott complimented with due enthusiasm and lavish praise—Gwen learned that he like to box and play racketball and that he had been on the rowing team in college. They had a spirited discussion about the various merits and failings of American poets and somehow wandered on to the subject of the history of the American Indian. She learned that his grandmother had been Welsh and that someone had traced his family tree—of course, Scott referred to it as Rick's family tree—back to the fourteenth century, when there were one duke, two traitors, an enterprising con artist and a witch. Gwen discovered that he had a weakness for saltwater taffy and a collection of Superman comic books. He like the big-band sound of the forties and western novels. Scott, of course, learned almost nothing about Gwen. It was a fact he noticed but did not push. He was afraid to let her guess how hungry he was to absorb everything about her, how impatient he was with her reluctance to share herself. He was grateful for each little tidbit she dropped, every movement and every smile and every expression in those brilliant, incredibly expressive eyes—anything that would open the door a little wider on who she was.

And because the rapport that was developing between them was so warm and so easy, Gwen did not feel awkward about asking him one thing that had been nagging at the back of her mind since he had first mentioned it. "What happened to the woman you were engaged to, Scott?" she inquired, taking the final, reluctant sip of her wine. She would have liked to have had another glass, but the fine vintage was potent.

Scott did not seem in the least disturbed by the question, and Gwen was glad. She did not want to think that the subject might still be a painful one for him. He merely seemed to be giving the question due consideration while he formulated his answer. "I don't want this to sound snobbish," he began, "but being in the position I was in wasn't always easy. There were groupies everywhere, and they would do anything to be able to say they had slept with someone close to Rick Stewart. As for his brother—" Scott shook his head a little, trying to hide a grin "—well," he admitted modestly, "you might say I was something of a prime target."

"But, of course," put in Gwen, her own eyes lightening with a twinkle, "being the perfect saint you are, you never took advantage of the situation."

Scott widened his eyes in mock insult. "Of course not." Then he grinned. "As a matter of fact, Rick would have had my hide if he had known some of the lengths I went to in order to take advantage of the situation. But, of course," he assured her gravely, "that was in the days of my wild, foolish youth. After I grew up a bit—" he shrugged "—it got to be a bore. And worse. It was hard to get a real date. The women that I might have liked to go out with weren't interested in all the media hype and security checks and often—" he lifted an eyebrow meaningfully at her "—they had prejudged me so much that I didn't have a chance. Then there were still those who, even though they pretended to be sophisticated, were impressed by nothing more than the status of the whole thing. Caroline—that's my ex-fiancée's name—fell somewhere between the two, I suppose. Hell, I was so happy to have found someone who would actually give me a chance that I fell head over heels in love, without thinking about it twice. I guess I rushed things a bit, and by the time she found out I wasn't as charismatic, talented or powerful as Rick, and by the time I found out she wasn't as wonderful as I first thought, it was too late—we were already engaged.'' And he cocked his head a little, thoughtfully. ''Happy ending, though. We were both a lot happier to get out of the engagement than we ever thought about being while we were engaged.''

Gwen smiled, but she thought it was a very sad story. How dreadful it must have been to put his trust in someone and then find it wasn't Scott she wanted after all, but his brother. What a lonely life he must have led. And how had he survived it all without growing cynical, bitter and suspicious? He was a very special person. Gwen realized that more and more with each passing minute.

Scott touched his napkin to his lips with a deep sigh of satisfaction for the meal and then demanded with a mischievous gleam, ''What's for dessert?''

Gwen told him, deadpan, ''I must have forgotten to make one.''

Scott widened his eyes in mock horror, and with a grin, Gwen rose to retrieve the chocolate mousse she had purchased from a specialty bak-

ery on her way home. In a single graceful movement, Scott was beside her, his hands upon her
waist, his thighs brushing her, the light of his eyes
taking her breath away. "Let me take care of dessert tonight," he said softly, and his mouth slowly
covered hers.

It was swift, it was unexpected, but it was what
Gwen had been waiting for since the first night
she met him. It was an easy melding as his tongue
slipped inside her mouth, an unquestioned opening to intimacy. It was all the softness and all the
fire that Gwen had known it would be, and still it
was more.

She rested her hands on his forearms, and at
first it was simply for support because surprise
took her breath away and the influx of tingling,
heart-speeding sensations made her knees weak.
She felt his lips clasp hers, lightly and with re-
straint; tentatively, he started to lift his face. But
that one taste, heady as it was, was not enough for
Gwen. Her tongue slipped out and traced the
curve of his lips; she felt the intake of his breath
as she tilted her mouth to better explore his. Her
hands crept up along his arms and rested on either
side of his neck; she could feel the heat of his skin
against her palms like a brand. And she was
drugged with the all-consuming sensation of his
mouth upon hers and hers upon his—tasting each
other, drawing from each other, giving life to each
other.

His fingers, when he slipped his hand under her
blouse, held her gently, not crushing her to him.
Sharing with her, not demanding of her. His fingertips were soft, and where they touched seemed

permanently electrified, as his hands traveled slowly down to caress her buttocks, holding her, cupping her. It was a natural gesture, smooth and easy, vaguely possessive, and Gwen did not mind. She wanted to be possessed by him. She already felt as though she were.

There should have been no great conflict. Her body was heating beneath his touch; her mind was filled with him. She wanted him. This kiss was the beginning, the threshold of pleasure so deep, the wonders so great, that she could not even imagine them. The touch of his tongue, the movements of his fingers, incited anticipation and filled her mind and her body with images that went beyond anything she had known: his skin, bare against hers; his long supple body stretched over hers, free to the exploration of her hands; his mouth upon her breasts, her abdomen, the sensitive flesh on the inside of her thighs; his fingers discovering her, her body welcoming him. They would be wonderful together. They *were* wonderful together.

Yet she must have known from the beginning there would be more to it than that—carefree eyes laughing at her on the beach, the lighthearted antics of a little boy, the quiet desperation of a man in pain. He had stumbled; she had helped him up, and from that moment something deep inside her had been touched. The only part of her he had not yet filled was her body. He had taken over her thoughts, her emotions, her time. He had moved within her feelings no one had ever explored before; feelings that no one had a right to explore. He made her think too much about herself— those compelling, unwavering eyes that demanded truths she was not even sure she knew, the gentle smile that understood the answers she could not give. And now he was asking more. More than just sex; that she would have given willingly. But what would happen to her when her body, as well as her mind, was committed to Scott Stewart? Would her heart soon follow?

His lips pulled gently away, and they touched her cheek. His hands slid slowly back up to her waist and folded there, fingers entwined against the exposed skin of her back. Within Gwen, demanding sexual impulses were turning her body to jelly: the flush of fever, the quivering just beneath the skin, the shallowness of breath, the crashing rhythm of her heart. She could feel his breath, too, short and heavy and hot against her neck, and his heartbeat strong against her breast. Very strong. There was that heavy, wavering sensation in the pit of her stomach and the almost irresistible compulsion to turn her face back to his, to drink in the taste of him, to take his hand and press it to her breast, to link arms with him and walk toward the bedroom, just a few steps away. So easy. So necessary. And so complicated.

His lips touched the corner of her eye; he looked down at her. "Wendy." There was a smile in his tone, but it was forced. And his voice was husky. "You know what we should do now, don't you?"

She looked up at him, her eyes wide and overbright, yet strangely deep in color. It was impossible to miss the messsage there. She whispered soberly, "Yes, I know."

Scott searched her eyes again and her face, and

he tried to shield his disappointment. "But," he said gently, with an effort, "I guess we're not going to."

Gwen closed her eyes, and she leaned against his shoulder again. It was the wrong thing to do, she knew. But she needed him—his warmth, his support. She needed him. That was perhaps the most disturbing thing of all. Scott had brought something special into her life and she had come to depend upon it. "It's so fast, Scott," she whispered. It was painful even to say. "And so important. It shouldn't be, but it is. I don't want to be sorry."

Scott dropped a kiss upon her hair, lifting one hand to stroke her back in silent reassurance. He was filled unexpectedly with a need for her so powerful it completely overshadowed the physical desire, so consuming it made him weak. Wendy. She filled him. She moved him deeply, profoundly. He did not deserve a thing as wonderful as she. He was terrified of losing it, or worse, of never having had it.

She was being cautious. That was good. He shouldn't be hurt. You were only careful of things that you cared about. She cared about him; now she was beginning to admit it to herself. He did not want to rush her. He didn't want to frighten her away. But he had to tell her.

"Wendy," he said softly. He lifted his hands to her face and cupped it, gently lifting it to his. She looked so confused, so vulnerable, so filled with need and reluctance, that he just wanted to fold her in his arms and kiss her until her doubts dissolved, to make love to her until she was sure. But he had to try with words instead. And it wasn't easy. "I know it hasn't been very long," he said. The struggle he was having putting this all into calm, precise words showed on his face. "I know there are things you don't understand about me...or even like about me." The instant denial that formed in her eyes caused his heart to flutter and leap with a soar of hope. "But, Wendy," he said quickly, before she could interrupt with something that might make him lose his nerve. "I want you to know that I care about you, a very, very great deal. It's something deeper than I've ever felt for anyone before, something special. I want to know you. I want to be close to you. I want to be a part of you. You make me want to be a better person, Wendy," he said simply. "And I guess that's the most special thing one person can do for another."

Gwen had to move her eyes away; the quiet, simple truth deep within him was causing something to ache and twist deep inside her. *You make me want to be better, too, Scott,* she thought, and the yearning inside her held an edge of despair. *Only I don't know if I have the courage.*

She looked back to him, her lips tipped upward briefly in an uncertain smile. She wanted there to be hope for them. She wanted him to help her find her courage. And she wanted most of all never, ever, to hurt him. "Just a little time, Scott," she whispered. Her hand reached up, and tentatively her fingertip traced the bristly outline of his sideburn, just as she had yearned to do since the first moment she saw him. He smiled at the gesture, and that encouraged her. "Okay?"

Scott looked at her—the china-doll face, the soft, embraceable body, the crystal-bright eyes. Like rainbows, those eyes—light was captured in arcs and colors and with it all a man's hopes, all his dreams. "Okay," he said huskily and smiled.

His hands still cupped her face; now he let his fingers sweep her hair behind her ears, tucking it there with a caress. He wanted to let his fingers drift down her throat, and across her shoulders, further to the pointed V of flesh and the soft round thrust of her breasts. The texture of her skirt had been wildly exciting in his hands; he wanted to feel more of it. So feminine, so alluring, she filled all his senses, sharpened all his needs, invaded every part of his mind, yet still left something, the most important thing, lacking.

He drew in a breath and released it shakily. Its warmth fluttered over Gwen's skin and she basked in it. "Pretty Wendy," he said softly, and he let his hands drop to her shoulders. His eyes went over her, reaching to her, pulling her, absorbing her and seemingly saddened by what he saw. "So many layers of you," he said, "and I want to know them all. Soft and lovely on the outside, all frills and lace. And beneath that you're a tough and efficient law officer with a gun on your hip and the light of righteousness in your eyes. But beneath that there's this beautiful woman, sexy and provocative and witty and sharp...and just a little bit unsure of herself. But beneath that—" he peered at her, as though he could answer the question for himself with his eyes alone "—what is there? What is at the center of Gwendolyn Blackshire?"

Gwen dropped her eyes and released a long breath. And she had to turn away from him. "I don't know, Scott," she said softly. "I really don't know."

And that, of course, was what frightened her most.

Chapter Ten

"You are just the slightest bit crazy, you know that?" Gwen brought another bucket of water and poured it carefully into the trough Scott had scraped with his hands.

"But a hell of an architect, right?" Scott carefully removed a bit of seaweed from the moat and sat back proudly to survey his work.

He had insisted upon building his castle far away from the tide line and on a bed of rock, so that all the water and a great deal of the sand had to be imported. And it was, indeed, a magnificent structure. Sprawling almost six feet long, a yard across and three stories high, it was multiturreted, double-fortified and many-windowed—a sand castle to end all sand castles.

They had spent the entire afternoon building it. It was Thursday, the first of Gwen's two days off, and it had begun with a surprise breakfast of croissants and oranges at seven-thirty that morning, when Scott had roused her from bed with the repeated ringing of her door bell, a deli bag in his hand and a cheerful smile on his face. On her days off Gwen liked to sleep late, and she had told him that, if it had not been for the deli bag, she probably wouldn't have let him in, but, of course, that wasn't true. All thoughts of sleep fled the moment she knew Scott was at the door. Even the croissants, which Gwen would normally have considered a highly insubstantial breakfast, were delicious and surprisingly filling.

Today they had shared the long-awaited picnic on the beach; that night Scott had promised her dinner at a highly touted restaurant thirty miles down the coast. Since they had gone no farther than the beach outside his house for the picnic, Gwen declared that she was highly deserving of a change of scenery, but she really didn't care. As long as she was with Scott, they could have been enclosed in a six-foot perimeter of barbed-wire fencing and she would not have minded. She wouldn't have minded a bit.

The last four days had not been easy. Gwen had seen Scott twice, both times for less than an hour for a walk on the beach or a short visit after dinner. Part of that was because of Gwen's schedule; part of it was because they each knew they were only torturing themselves, being together but not being together. The sexual tension between them was palpable, Gwen's uncertainty wavering and fluctuating like the tides of the moon. He called every night, and once they had talked for two hours. It was midnight at the end of that conversation, and once again Gwen wrestled with the mind-defeating urge to ask him to come over—just to come to her, to be with her, to stay with her. But instead, she had said a soft good night and afterward lay for a long time in her bed, sleepless, feeling very, very stupid.

Gwen usually wasn't this cautious about relationships. Usually she knew they wouldn't last and she didn't much want them to. Usually all she was looking for was companionship, a few good times, someone not too dull and not too demanding, to fill her spare hours. No emotional investment, no great expectations, just something short and pleasant, with an uncomplicated parting at the end of a few weeks. Scott was different. God knew she didn't want him to be, and she could not explain to herself why, but he was. And that was what made her so unsure.

Over and over she told herself she was crazy. She replayed the meeting on the beach, hoping to generate some disgust or, better yet, some smug superiority touched with just a twinge of pity for him. It didn't work. He had been more than drunk and helpless that night; he had been human. He had been open, vulnerable and real. No defenses, no pretenses, just Scott. Perhaps that was why he had gotten to her so deeply and so quickly. He had had nothing to hide; he had given her all he had without reservation and that had bonded her to him, somehow. It was a rare thing to know someone so deeply so quickly.

But what did she really know about him? Repeatedly Gwen barraged herself with that accusation. There were a lot of pieces, none of them holding together to form the real man—uncertain images, waving back and forth, none of them forming a clear picture of the man Scott Stewart would be when he was in charge of his own life. How could she hold on to something like that?

And why did she want to?

"Not bad, for a sand castle," she admitted now, sitting back on her heels to survey it. "A little on the gaudy side."

Scott shot her a defensive look. "Intricate, my dear, is the word," he corrected haughtily. "Or perhaps, merely awesome." He made a slight adjustment to one of the tower windows. "Yes," he decided in satisfaction. "Awesome."

Gwen glanced at him, her eyes dancing merrily from beneath shaded lashes. He looked wonderful today, his hair tossed by the wind, his eyes crinkled with the sun. He was wearing white shorts and a pullover shirt; the sleeves of his nylon Windbreaker were pushed up to his elbows as he worked. Gwen was drawn again and again to the line of lean muscles from calf to thigh, as he rested his weight on one knee beside the castle. The light covering of hair on his legs gleamed reddish-gold in the sunlight, the flesh lightly tanned, the shape hard. She wanted to trail her hand along those muscles. She had been wanting to do it all day.

She said, "I don't know why it had to be so big. You're going to make all the other kids on the block jealous."

"It's not big," he objected. "It's grand. Nothing but the best for the summer home of Princess Gwendolyn of Blackshire."

She laughed, surprise mingling with embarrassment on her cheeks, and he continued seriously, "Notice the careful attention to detail Her Highness's royal builder has put into the construction of this magnificent retreat. Double walls," he pointed out, "to protect against invaders. Three enclosed gardens in which Her Loveliness can stroll in the moonlight. A freshwater moat by which to dream on long summer days. And—" he touched a tiny window high atop the most prominent tower "—a balcony outside her bedroom, from which she can be serenaded by her lover." He cast a shaded glance at her. "And—" his finger trailed down "—a series of artfully concealed block steps by which the ingenious lover can climb up to Her Highness's royal waiting arms."

Something strange bubbled through Gwen with the delicately shielded look in his lightly fringed eyes, the note of suggestive musing in his voice, and it found its outlet in nervous laughter. "You are crazy," she decided, and then slapped his thigh playfully, leaping to her feet. "Come on, let's get some exercise. You've been lolling around on the beach doing nothing all day!"

"You call building a magnificent fourteenth-century structure nothing?" he retorted, indignant, but she was already running down the beach, and it did not take him long to catch up.

They ran together until the beach became too rocky, and Gwen laughed when Scott became winded first. "See what building magnificent fourteenth-century structures does for you?" she teased him, and they linked hands as they started walking back down the beach. "Nothing! No muscle tone, no circulatory stress—"

"I'll show you muscle tone!" Without warning he grabbed her by the waist and lifted her high in the air. Gwen could not prevent a squeak of surprise as she found herself looking down into those sparkling green eyes, the flushed face, the soft lips parted for laughing breath...and then the gentling of those eyes, the steady constriction of his arms as she was lowered by inches until her lips touched his, softly, sweetly. Her hands braced against his shoulders, and she felt the wave of soft, tingling heat rise over her as his lips touched and nibbled at hers—clasping, parting, turning, teasing, making her ache for more. Her tongue darted to explore his inner lip, and his breath was short and uneven as it mingled with hers, but Gwen could no longer be sure it was from the exercise. It was a delicious torture, this light, exploratory, deliberately teasing magic of his mouth and tongue. Gwen wanted to press herself close to him and demand more, but he held her firmly at a distance, with her feet a few inches off the ground. The stretch-knit top she wore had slid up when he grabbed her, and two of his fingers were clasping her bare waist. Just two fingers, but it was maddening.

And then she felt her feet resting gently and fully on solid ground; he wrapped his arms around her. She tilted her face upward to receive the full pressure of his mouth, but he bent his head and rested his face against her hair, just holding her. His heart was beating solidly and steadily; his breathing was slow and controlled. Gwen's arms were entwined around his waist, and it was all she could do to keep from tightening her grip, from crushing him to her and thereby communicating the desperate depth of her need. His tenderness filled her and weakened her, and her response to it swelled within her until she was almost blind from needing him. Scott—gentle, whimsical, tender, poetic—the dreamer and the lover. All the things she was not. It frightened Gwen to think how much she wanted him in her life. It stunned her to think how much he meant to her. And the yearnings that filled her when he held her in his arms like this were so much more than physical. They were so powerful that they were almost desperate.

His hands moved upward to her shoulders, caressing, holding. He stepped back a fraction, but he did not release her. Instead, he looked down at her, his face filled with tenderness, yet sober; his eyes were crystal-clear on the surface but opaque as they probed deep into her soul, absorbing her. "I love you, Wendy," he said softly.

For a moment even Gwen's breathing was paralyzed, captured in the depths of his eyes, in the quiet tenor of his words. But before understanding or rejection or even hope could form on her face, the moment was gone. Scott controlled it; he closed it with a smile and turned to slip his arm casually around her waist.

"It's about time we got ready for dinner," he said easily, and they started walking back toward the cliff steps. "Why don't you wait for me while I change, and then I'll take you back to your house. The place we're going to does not hold reservations," he assured her, and the spark in his eyes was warm and relaxed.

Gwen thought she nodded and agreed, and she also thought her smile must have been a little strained, her face somewhat stunned. She did not participate very much in the conversation as they went back to Scott's house, and even when he had left her in the living room with a glass of wine while he went to shower, her mind was still far away from the designer-decorated beach house, the taste of expensive wine, the comfortable sofa on which she sat. Most of her was still back on the beach, tossed by the gentle winds, captured in the depths of Scott's eyes.

I love you, Wendy. Why should everything seem so simple when he said those words? Deep and meaningful and important words. She had heard them before. *I love you, sweetheart,* from her father. *Love ya, kid,* from Tim, after she had gotten her hands on prize tickets to a football game or *I love you, babe,* from one of the officers when she volunteered for double shift so he could have the day off. And she had heard them under other, less sincere circumstances. *I love you* meant the sex was good. *I love you* meant the meal was enjoyable or thanks for the beer or you sure look good in that low-necked dress. But when Scott said, *I love you, Wendy,* it meant exactly what he said. It meant the whole world was different.

Was that it, then? Was that the key to the whole thing? *I love you, too, Scott.* But how could that be? What could she know about love in just two weeks; how could she love a man who could not be defined; how could she love someone else when she was not certain how much she even loved herself? So easy to say, so easy to feel... like a light that was swelling and intensifying deep within her, a truth that simply refused to be denied, blotting out all the shadowy corners where uncertainty lurked.

Maybe it was love. She was very afraid that it was love. It was the reason he had haunted her every waking moment since the day she met him, the reason her stomach tightened and her heart beat faster every time she saw him; it was what made her smile when he did and hurt when she saw the shadow of sadness cross his eyes. It was what made her angry when she saw him wasting his life; it was what made her care about the mistakes he was making; it was what made her so very intensely involved with him. It was something that she simply couldn't help, and it frightened her as much as it thrilled her. She didn't want to love Scott. She didn't want the kind of intense emotional attachment that would only build up their dreams and shatter them both when they discovered how different they really were. Simple, practical Gwen knew better than to let this thing get out of hand. And now, of course, it was too late. It was already out of hand.

When Scott came out of the bathroom, Gwen was waiting for him in the bedroom. If he was surprised, or even shocked, he dismissed it with a grin and challenged, "What, a beautiful princess in my boudoir? Doesn't she know how to knock?"

"Princesses don't have to knock," she retorted, an easy smile tightening the corners of her lips. "Besides," she pointed out, "I believe I've seen you in a greater state of—shall we say—dishabille?"

His grin deepened and his eyes sparkled with it,

but beneath the light demeanor, he was searching her face, questioningly, a little uncertainly. He was wearing a loosely belted maroon robe and had a navy towel around his neck; moisture glistened on the bare V of his chest and darkened the hair on his legs. His hair was more wet than dry, slightly disheveled by a brisk toweling and a careless straightening with his fingers. He was strong, sexy and shower-fresh; he brought into the room with him the scent of humid air and spicy soap, and all of him assaulted Gwen's senses on a very primitive level.

On his bed were arranged a blue silk shirt and a dark suit. The shirt had French cuffs. He would be devastating in that outfit—sleek, continental, sophisticated, a side of Scott Gwen had never seen before. But right now, in the soft velour robe, with his wet hair, and with his bare feet leaving damp imprints in the carpet, he was the Scott Gwen knew best: casual, unaffected, unashamed. Her Scott.

He went to retrieve his clothes with an nonchalant stride that Gwen suspected might hide a touch of nervousness. He tossed over his shoulder, "What can I do for you, pretty lady?"

And Gwen heard herself respond, "Kiss me."

Scott let the shirt and suit he had half lifted fall back to the bed. He straightened up and turned, the slow light in his eyes sweeping her and examining her, welcoming her, yet questioning. "We might not make our reservation," he suggested softly.

At first Gwen did not know why she had come in here—to talk to him, she supposed, to be with him for a minute while these new and uncontrollably confusing emotions and ideas were fighting their way for acceptance within her. Now she knew exactly why she had come. "I don't care," she answered and stepped into his arms.

To Gwen, unused to dealing with complexities, it was the only thing to do. She wanted him; she needed him with every part of her, not just her body. The compulsion was too powerful to be fought for long; she did not know why she had even tried. They wanted one another, they were ready to share with one another, they would have one another. Nothing could be simpler.

But she was unprepared for what the feel of Scott's hands upon her bare flesh would do to her—the touch of his lips in all those secret places, the length of his body, strong and hard, brushing against hers, wrapping itself around hers. There were sensations, familiar, aching, body-tightening sensations; there was the mindless excitement of discovery, the breathless, heated rise of passion, the shaky weakness of a new experience, but there was more. There was something that filled her whole mind, that invaded every cell of her being, that washed through her and left her forever changed. It was Scott. Not just making love. Making love with Scott. He was her heartbeat; he was her breath; he was every particle of life within her. And she was too in awe, too filled with that blinding light of love and fulfillment that was Scott even to be frightened by it.

It wasn't wild and fiery and uncontrollable sex. It was long and slow and heartbreakingly intense love. It was not what he did for her, or what she did for him, but what they created together. His entry into her body was gentle and easy, yet it shook the very foundation of the world. It took away her breath in one huge gasp and left her motionless, everything within her stilled in concentration: the reddish-orange shadows of the sunset that played across his skin, the quiet look of deep rapture in his heavily lidded eyes, the touch of his lips upon her hair, the gentle, soothing motions of his fingertips as they stroked her cheeks. Love. It filled her.

In retrospect the images that lingered in Gwen's mind were like scraps of poetry: the shape of his body as he stretched over her, gently holding her wrists above her head as he availed himself of the taste of her throat and her ears and her breasts; the lean planes of his back and the curve of his arms beneath her reverent fingertips, the tantalizing brush of his chest against her breasts; his mouth covering hers, his tongue mating with hers; the silky feel of his stubby lashes as she brushed her fingertips across them, his fleeting smile when she did that; the shadow on the wall as he straightened his arms and arched his body into her, easing deeper and deeper; his face, so beautiful, so adoring—and so adored.

Twilight had fallen in earnest when Scott at last held her, curled up into his arms and legs as close as she could get, her small hand spread upon his chest, her closed lashes shadowing her cheeks. How small she looked now, how doll-like and fragile, how intensely vulnerable, and how his heart swelled to bursting with love for her. Pretty Wendy, ephemeral, delicate, touchable but un-

holdable. Complex layers hiding secret depths.
Could she ever belong to him?

Was it too soon for you, love, he worried. *Did I
rush you into something you weren't ready to give? I
didn't mean to. I would have waited forever. Oh,
Wendy, ask me what I want from you now. No, don't
ask me. I'm afraid I might tell you.*

He wondered if she knew how much she could
hurt him now. So long used to protecting himself,
Scott had had no thought of guarding himself
against the one person who could do him more
damage than anyone else in his life. And now it
was too late. He would never stop wanting her. He
would never stop needing her, all of her. And
there was no guarantee that she would give him
what he needed, what he could no longer live
without. He wondered if even he knew how much
she could hurt him.

Gwen lay within the shelter of his arms, her
eyes closed, but she was not asleep. Scott was still
in every part of her, the taste of his lips on her
tongue, the moisture of his body on her skin, the
throb of his ardor in her veins. The mingling of
his essence was within her mind, and a part of him
lodged deep within her soul. Something had happened to her. She was not the same person she
had been when she stepped into this bedroom.
She was no longer a separate person with individual needs and problems and joys; she was a part of
another, and he of her. She didn't belong to herself anymore, yet she felt freer than she ever had
in her life. She wanted to tell Scott. She wanted to
tell him that this was special, this was different,
that never had anything like this happened to her

before. She did not understand it, but she didn't want to fight it; she simply wanted to revel in it, to share it with him.

But it was all too new and too complicated, and it was too soon for her to absorb it. She could not even put it into words. She could only say that, for this moment, she was happier than she had ever been in her life, and she felt like flying.

Gwen opened her eyes. Her forefinger traced a slow circle around Scott's nipple; she felt his flesh, sated and languorously warm, begin to prickle with the motion. He glanced down at her. "What're you doing, witch?" he murmured.

"Witch or princess? Make up your mind."

Gwen's voice was husky and bubbly; even the sound of it ignited new awareness into the wonderful veil of lethargy that was descending upon Scott. "All things to all men," he responded, and the mock insult that widened her eyes delighted him.

Quickly, he apologized, burying his grin in her hair, "I meant, of course, all things to one man."

She accepted the apology somewhat grumpily. "That's better." The spark in her eyes was mischievous as she glanced up at him again. "Go ahead," she invited. "Say it."

He smiled down at her indulgently as he placed another light kiss on her hair. "Say what?" He loved the fragrance of her hair and the texture— too thick and too shiny to be real. He could spend hours doing nothing but caressing her hair.

"Was it good for you, too, baby?" she mimicked throatily, and he lay back against the pillows, chuckling.

One arm encircled her shoulders, the other rested across his forehead. He shot her a look of amused reprimand from beneath the shelter of his arm as he returned, "Tacky, tacky. I thought you had more class than that, Officer Blackshire." After a silence he inquired, "Was it?"

"Fair," she allowed. He had never noticed before how deep her dimples were when she smiled. They enchanted him. "How about you?" she asked.

Scott turned his eyes back to the ceiling. "Actually," he confessed, "I was a little disappointed. I seem to distinctly recall the planet splitting in two at some point, but here we are, lying in bed, and nothing looks any different to me. I must have imagined it."

"Must have," agreed Gwen soberly, her eyes dancing. *I love you,* she thought. *I love you so much.*

Abruptly, Scott rolled her over on her back, his weight resting on his elbows, his legs straddling hers, his chest and abdomen fitting against hers. His eyes were alive with delight and humor, sending out little sparks that caught in hers and doubled back to him. "Maybe we should try it again, just to find out."

"You deserve a chance to improve on 'fair,'" she agreed soberly, and encircled his neck with her arms.

For the first time in her life, Gwen forgot about dinner.

Chapter Eleven

Scott opened his eyes to a hazy dawn, and her face filled his vision. At first he started to drift off to sleep again, knowing it was only another dream. And then it stole over him, the truth of it, the wonder of it, and for a moment the emotions that filled him were so powerful that he could not breathe.

Gwen had been awake since the first gray light crept into the shadowy corners of the room, watching him. She had awakened with a golden peace inside her that felt like a wonderful secret, and by watching him, she had tried to keep that beauty from dissolving into the harsh edges of doubt that were inevitable with the coming of day. It was a fairy tale, she knew. Lady Gwendolyn and her Prince Charming. They could not hold on to this. Too soon their differences would tear them apart; too soon the things yet undiscovered about themselves and each other would come between them; too soon they would have to face the fact that they had only been making believe. Gwen did not have long-term relationships. She knew that. But she knew that the ending of this one was going to tear her apart, and the knowledge filled her with a dread and despair like none she had ever known. She didn't want it to end. She did not want to face the reasons why it must.

She saw Scott's eyes open, sweet and unfocused and hazy with sleep; she saw the misty wonder fill them and it pulled her, slowly, unresistingly, toward the source of her joy. He smiled at her; one warm finger reached up to trace the outline of her jaw. "What are you thinking about?" he whispered.

"Cupid," she answered. His touch spread over her skin like warm honey. "You look like Cupid when you sleep."

"Ah, yes." His voice was airy and husky, his smile as warm as the sun upon water. "The classic tale wherein it is proved beyond a doubt that love cannot live with uncertainty." Why did it surprise her so much that he knew the story? Why did it fill her with such unexpected pleasure? His hands slipped beneath the covers and fastened on her waist; with a single graceful movement he shifted her on top of him. Yet his smile seemed to fade a little, and his eyes were serious as he inquired, "Are you still uncertain of me, Wendy?"

She wanted to tell him she was not. She could feel his body beneath hers, warm and strong and enveloping her. She wanted to believe in this. She wanted him inside her, and she wanted to hold him there forever. She wanted all of him and she wanted it desperately.

But she looked at him, clear-eyed and soberly, and she knew she could tell him none of those things. "Are you certain of me, Scott?" she asked softly.

Scott looked at her for a long time; then he slowly drew her head down onto his shoulder. *No,* he thought, reluctantly, bleakly. *No, God help me, I'm not. I'm not certain of anything anymore.*

So he held her, quietly and surely, until their bodies began to arrange themselves into the instinctive movements of love. The morning light filled the room with questions they could not answer and chose not to ask.

TWO HOURS LATER Scott was leaning against the wall of the kitchen, looking grumpy and sleepy; Gwen was busily and somewhat futilely examining the contents of his refrigerator. "Do you have any idea what time it is?" Scott complained.

"Yogurt!" exclaimed Gwen, horrified. "Your refrigerator is filled with nothing but yogurt!"

"You're impossible in the morning," Scott grumbled, and Gwen sidled up to him, her straying hands invoking responses he would have thought himself incapable of after his recent exertions, her magical eyes piercing arrows of need straight into his soul.

"Am I?" she teased, and he captured her hand drawing a sharp breath. "God, yes," he said weakly, and she laughed, flitting away from him.

She poured a cup of coffee, nodding toward the refrigerator. "You realize, of course," she informed him, "that yogurt is a poor excuse for the breakfast you promised me."

"Sorry," he returned lightly. "I wasn't expecting overnight guests. Especially—" and his eyes twinkled at her wickedly ''—those with insatiable appetites.''

Gwen chose not to respond to that, but instead watched him pour spoonfuls of sugar and half a cup of milk into his cup, with a skeptically lifted eyebrow. ''How about a little coffee in your cream and sugar, Mr. Stewart?'' she suggested, and he grinned.

''Okay, so my ideas on good nutrition end at yogurt,'' he admitted. He took a long sip of the lukewarm mixture and set the coffee cup down decisively, striding toward the door. He plucked Gwen's jacket from the hook were she had left it yesterday and tossed it to her. Gwen caught it in astonishment.

''What are you doing, kicking me out over a little disagreement about breakfast?''

''Nope.'' His eyes twinkled as he slung his own jacket over his shoulder and brushed a kiss across her nose. ''Feeding you.''

Gwen feasted on hotcakes and sausages at a diner several miles down the coast; Scott, perversely, ordered yogurt. They laughed and they teased each other, and the rising sun sparkled off the rugged Pacific rocks like diamond chips. They stopped at a twenty-four-hour market and picked up supplies for lunch and dinner—enough, Scott pointed out dryly, to feed a football team for a week, and they took a meandering route along the coastal highway back to his house. The sun had never been more brilliant, the sky clearer, the ocean more mesmerizing. And Scott's presence was like a warm glow that penetrated her from the inside out, spreading and buoying her and sealing everything in a golden glow. It was being in love—the magic, the euphoria, the crazy chemical and emotional imbalance that had caused poets for centuries to liken the condition to insanity. Gwen knew that, but it did not make it any less wonderful. It was so easy, in this unbelievably happy state, to imagine that it would last forever, to push the problems and the conflicts far, far away. The day was wonderful, Scott was wonderful, and Gwen was the luckiest woman alive. If anything could possibly go wrong, she did not want to know about it.

They returned to the house just before ten and Scott, still complaining about the early awakening, decided a nap was in order. Gwen, who wasn't the least bit sleepy, went with him.

It was a little after noon when Gwen's eyes, on an automatic signal from her stomach, flickered open again. On synchronization, Scott's eyes opened a crack, and he smiled and stretched his arms overhead. "What a way to spend a day," he murmured and lowered his arms to shelter her again.

Gwen pushed an insistent forefinger into his sternum; Scott flinched but did not open his eyes. "I'm—"

"I know. Hungry." With unexpected swiftness for one who had only seconds ago appeared to be drifting back to sleep, Scott moved over her, his hands pinning her shoulders, and nudged his legs between hers. His eyes were glass-bright. "We may have a little problem with that," he informed her, and his lips dropped to nibble at her neck. "I seem to have this uncontrollable appetite myself." A trail of electricity followed the sweeping path of his tongue across her chest. "For you."

"Scott." She drew in her breath as his teeth lightly clasped her nipple, tongue teasing, flaring tingling sensations in radiating sparks to every part of her skin. Her hand crept around his shoulder. "I'm not sure how long we can go on behaving like this."

"My physical prowess amazes me," he agreed modestly, and swept his attention to her other breast. Heat flared like a rising flush throughout Gwen's body, and she was no longer thinking about lunch.

What began as playful lovemaking quickly grew serious as it always did with them. Gwen could feel the urgency rising within her as he dipped his head to explore with his tongue the sweep of her torso and the slight convexity of her abdomen, physical demand coupled with something more— just the need for him, to be wrapped within him, to be joined with him again, just one more time, for however long. Gwen could feel the quickening of his breath and the rising temperature of his skin against her fingers and against her lips as she placed deep, tasting kisses over his shoulders and his chest. Then he gathered her to him, his face buried in her neck, and she could feel the slight quivering of his muscles when he whispered hoarsely, "I just can't seem to get enough of you."

Nor I, you, Gwen thought, and she wrapped her arms more tightly around him, her lips traveling across his face and his neck, urging him to complete the union. The hot-sweet surge of passion was swirling again, blinding them, sealing them into the exclusive world of heartbeats and breaths and touches and responses. Neither heard the crunch of tires on the drive. Neither heard the front door close or heavy footsteps traverse the hall. Neither knew anything at all until a sharp "Ahem" from the doorway intruded into the soft sounds of their sighs.

At first it did not register. Gwen opened her eyes languorously; she saw above Scott's shoulder the figure of a man at the bedroom door, in sports coat and loosened tie, with rumpled dark hair and perfectly blank eyes. She gasped, and Scott's head swiveled around sharply; she grabbed the covers over her as he rolled away from her.

"When you're finished," said the man, deadpan, "I'd like to talk to you for a few minutes."

He turned and left, closing the door behind him.

For a time they just stared, shocked and speechless, and Gwen felt the slow flush of utter humiliation creep from her toes all the way up her body. Scott was breathing unevenly beside her, as motionless as she was, and from very far away came the sounds of the intruder moving around the living room, pouring himself a drink, making himself at home in Scott's house.

Then Scott said in a rather strangulated voice, "Would you hit me if I started to laugh?"

She turned shock-darkened, accusation-filled eyes on him, and he couldn't hold it back any longer. The restrained chuckles that had been shaking his shoulders broke through into helpless laughter; he lifted a hand to defend himself even before she threw the pillow.

"What the hell do you think is so funny? Of all the embarrassing ... humiliating ... debasing—"

"I object to debasing!" he managed, trying to duck another onslaught from the pillow.

"Things that could ever happen to a person! I've never ... ! What are you laughing at? Who was that man? How can you laugh?"

"Stop—don't!" He caught her wrists as the situation threatened to get out of hand, his eyes still dancing crazily. "I'm sorry, love, I really am— don't do that. Settle down." He tightened his hold as she tried to wrench away, and attempted a sober face. It didn't work. "It's only Lyle," he explained. "Listen, don't be mad. This only proves one thing." She looked at him suspiciously and he hastened to elaborate. "That I never have been known to entertain women in my bedroom in the middle of the day; otherwise Lyle would be used to knocking by now."

Reluctantly, Gwen had to admit that made a strange sort of sense, and she was mollified enough for Scott to release her wrists. But then a new wave of hot embarrassment flooded her, and she buried her face in the pillow, moaning lowly. Scott patted her shoulder reassuringly, but Gwen had an unpleasant suspicion that he was still laughing. His hand rested on her back, and when she ventured a glance at him again, he was lying back against the pillows, no longer laughing, only the smallest trace of rueful amusement still lingering in his eyes. "I suppose," he said, "I might as well go see what he wants." And then the wicked spark ignited in his eyes again as he cast her a quick glance. "I don't know about you," he said, "but I think I'm finished."

He dodged her last attack with the pillow and rolled off the bed. He was still laughing as he pulled on his clothes.

Ten minutes later Gwen, fully dressed, hair brushed, chin held high, responded to the insistent pressure of Scott's hand upon her elbow and entered the living room where Lyle waited. It had taken Scott every bit of those ten minutes to convince her to come out and properly meet his guest. In the end she only agreed because he teasingly accused her of cowardice.

Lyle Williams accepted the introduction and greeted her just as though their previous meeting had been in a grand ballroom instead of a bedroom. Now that she had a chance to really look at him, Gwen recognized him immediately from the party—he was the man who had finally succeeded in dragging Scott outside to the deck, the man who had refused to chase him down the cliff to the beach. Somehow she felt a little warmer toward Lyle after remembering that; if he had gone after Scott, she never would have, and everything would have been different. She was foolish enough then to be grateful for that.

When the amenities were served, Lyle did not allow the moment to become awkward. He went immediately to the point of his visit—or intrusion, however one chose to look at it. "You wanted me to keep you up to date on the Hampstead case," he said to Scott abruptly.

Scott lowered himself to the hassock at Gwen's

feet, resting a hand casually on her knee. "Great," he said. "What's up?"

Lyle passed an uncomfortable look at Gwen. "I know this isn't a good time," he said. "This is really something we should discuss in private."

Gwen started to rise, but a pressure of Scott's hand kept her seated. "It's all right," he told Lyle. "Wendy knows all about it. The lawsuit," he explained to her.

Lyle's expression was not inviting. "She doesn't know this," he said pointedly.

Scott released an exasperated breath. "Stop talking so much like a lawyer and get on with it. We haven't had lunch yet. Do you want to stay?"

"No, no." Lyle busied himself with shuffling some papers in his briefcase; then he stopped and looked directly at Scott. His face was very sober, his tone heavy. "You wanted an investigation," he said, "and you got it. But you're not going to like it."

Gwen glanced quickly at Scott, a measure of amazement filtering through her. He had asked for an investigation? He had become actively involved in what he had heretofore ignored? A small thread of wonder and pride wove its way to the surface, and she wanted to reach out and clasp his hand. But the expression on Scott's face stopped her.

His brows were knotted ominously. "What do you mean, I won't like it?"

Lyle released a pent-up breath; he stood up and began pacing in a taut, very controlled manner around the room. That was when Gwen knew something was wrong. Very wrong. Already she could feel the chill shadow of reality spreading its wings over their honey-golden day. "We've decided to settle out of court," Lyle said in a moment.

Gwen could feel the alertness within Scott, in his muscles, in his eyes, in his voice. "Why?" he inquired, wrestling to keep his own indignation under control. "Why do something like that when we can take it to court and put an end to this Hampstead creep and all the others like him. I don't want a settlement," he insisted belligerently. "That was the whole point. I want to make an example out of him. What makes you think you can just decide not to go to court?"

It was a short moment, but one crackling with intensity—will battling will, old authority versus new, tempers rising and subdued. Lyle took out a cigarette and lighted it with a jerky motion; the sound of the lighter snapped through the air. Then Lyle turned abruptly, his eyes very sharp. "Because," he said distinctly, "it's true."

Gwen would remember forever every detail of that scene: Lyle's tense, hunched form, the way his knuckles pressed an outline into the material of his slacks as he shoved his fists into his pockets; the way the day seemed suddenly still around them, even the sounds of the ocean muted, the bright splotch of sunshine on the hardwood floor, almost obscene in its gaiety; the blank incomprehension in Scott's eyes.

Scott said, with very little expression at all, "What's true? What do you mean?"

"Dammit, they have the originals!" In an abrupt explosion of impotent noise and activity,

Lyle strode back to the coffee table and jerked out several sheets of paper from his briefcase. "Hampstead was no fool—he sent copies of the songs by certified mail to himself. He was never paid a cent for them. They were published under Rick's name. For God's sake, how much clearer can it get?"

Scott took the papers from him with fingers that seemed peculiarly lifeless; his face was perfectly blank. Gwen felt the airless ache of shock in her own stomach gradually disperse into something more real, equally as painful. Rick Stewart, the saint of the entertainment world... Rick Stewart, the musical genius... Rick Stewart, philanthropist, common man, benevolent, honest, a hero among heroes... Rick Stewart would have been no more than another small-time hopeful if it hadn't been for material he had stolen from another man.

Scott rose slowly and walked away from her, still staring at the photocopies in his hand. Gwen reached for him but couldn't touch him. She let her hand trail away and looked helplessly into the raw pain in Lyle Williams's eyes. "I... don't understand," she said, a little weakly. "All this was so many years ago. Why wait until now to sue?"

With an effort Lyle dragged his eyes away from Scott and focused on her question. He released his breath in an uneven sigh. He took a nervous draw on the cigarette and snubbed it out with several swift, sloppy motions in a china ashtray. "Ah, hell," he muttered. He dragged his hand through his hair, and Gwen was aware of the way he avoided her eyes and Scott's; his words were mumbled to the center of the room. "We'd been paying him off," he said. "After Rick started to make it, Hampstead wanted in on the action. Well, Rick hadn't established his credibility yet, and he was afraid Hampstead would cause a scandal. He didn't know anything about the music business then, and I guess it seemed easier to him just to keep the man quiet rather than to share the glory. From the first payment, of course, it started to escalate and eventually got out of hand. The bigger Rick got, the more impossible it became for him to admit he'd made a mistake and just cut the whole thing off." Now he shot a glance at Gwen that was almost entreating. "He had his image to protect, you know."

Scott had said nothing; he had not even moved. Gwen looked at him, and there was nothing on his face even to indicate he had heard the confession. He simply stood by the fireplace and stared at the papers, but Gwen could sense the angry lashes of hurt and denial coiling within him.

Gwen felt a powerful urge to protect him, to close off the truth that Lyle was revealing, to shelter him from it. But there was nothing she could do. She heard herself saying to Lyle instead, very quietly, "And now that Rick is dead . . ."

"We tried to get Hampstead to sign a release," responded Lyle, "which is what should have been done in the first place. When he wouldn't, we stopped payments. He responded with the lawsuit." Now Lyle turned to Scott, and a muscle in his face twitched in reaction to Scott's pain. "Dammit, Scott," he said harshly, almost defensively, "you wanted to get involved. You wanted

to handle things. Well, this is what you're involved in, and I can't help it if it isn't pretty. I tried
to keep it from you. I told you we could take care
of this, but, no, you wouldn't have it. Dammit,
why couldn't you have just stayed out of it?''

"But are you—" Gwen started to say "sure,"
but she let the word fall unspoken. Of course he
was sure. The attorneys of a corporation as powerful as this one would not be duped. Lyle would
not have brought it up had he not been sure. This
was no powder-puff, cotton-candy world where
men played delicate games with each other; this
was real life, and legends fell with a mighty crash
every day. But none so mighty as this.

Scott spoke very lowly into the silence. "It's
not true," he said simply and without expression. He met Lyle's eyes levelly, and his face was
very white. His eyes looked like charcoal-green
smudges. "It's just not true."

Lyle took a step toward him. "Scott—"

"You've made a mistake," Scott continued,
just as calmly. "This is a setup. You know Rick.
You know he would never have done anything
like this. He never made a dishonest move in his
life. Everybody knows Rick Stewart. Nobody will
believe this." But deep down inside, Scott did believe it, he did know it was true, and that writhing flicker of pain in his eyes tore at Gwen's
heart.

Lyle approached Scott carefully. "Look, it's not
as bad as it seems. Nobody ever has to know
about this. If we put the right pressure in the right
places, settle enough on him, we can destroy the
evidence and nothing will ever come out. It will be

just as if it never happened—if you let us handle this."

"Shut up!" Scott shouted suddenly. His voice crashed through the stillness of the April afternoon. His face went wild; he flung the papers toward Lyle, and they scattered with a sweeping motion in the air. "Shut up and get out of here!" he spat out. "You're a liar! A vicious, ungrateful liar and you—" His voice broke suddenly on a dragged-in sound; the silence in its wake was sharp and as ringing as crystal. He turned away abruptly, his elbow propped against the mantel, his mouth resting upon his fist. The sound of his breathing was ragged.

Lyle stood there for a moment, looking at him helplessly. "Dammit, Scott," he said softly. "Why did you want to get involved in this anyway? Why did you have to be so curious?" And he turned away, a heavy sigh escaping him as he gathered up his briefcase. "Why couldn't I lie to you?"

Lyle turned back to Scott for one more bleak, sorrowful moment; then he nodded his good-bye to Gwen and left.

Gwen did not move; she did not speak. She let Scott have this time to absorb, to adjust, to try to understand. And her heart was breaking for him.

What must it be like to love a person as intensely as Scott had loved his brother, and then to discover all he had loved had been a lie? Scott Stewart had devoted his entire life to his brother. He had worshiped at the shrine of the legend even more intensely than the millions of strangers who had first claim on Rick Stewart. There had been more for Scott to worship because he knew the

legend better than anyone else; he was a part of it.
Scott was an extension of Rick; Rick was Scott's
whole life, more than a brother—a parent, a men-
tor, a protector, a role model, a hero, just as he
had been to three-quarters of the civilized world,
a pure and unsullied hero. The last of his kind.
And now the hero was dead, in a way more final
and absolute than the plane crash that had taken
his life a year ago. And Scott had to face the fact
that he had never known his brother at all. He had
given his life to an image, and the illusion was
gone.

At last Scott moved. He released a shaky breath
and pushed himself away from the mantel, only to
lean against the wall, his eyes closed, his head tilted
back helplessly. Something deep within Gwen
twisted for him. Had she done this? Had she
brought him this pain? If she hadn't insisted upon
his taking responsibility for his brother's business, if she hadn't interfered . . . Wouldn't it have
been better if he had never known? Lyle would
have handled it; he would have covered it up
neatly, and no one would ever have known. The
image would have stood untarnished; Scott would
have gone on believing. Shouldn't she have left
well enough alone?

Gwen got up and crossed over to him hesitantly. "Scott." She touched his arm. "Do you—
would you like me to leave you alone?"

She did not want him to say yes. She wanted
him to reach for her in times of sorrow as he did
in times of joy; she wanted to share this with him,
to soothe him if she could. But she knew there
was nothing she could do. There were times when

a person had to be alone with himself, had to face the demon inside him and conquer it, and no one could help.

Scott opened his eyes slowly, and it was a long time before he focused on her. "Yeah," he said lowly, at last, "I think so." His eyes shifted to the distant window. He took a breath and released it unsteadily.

Gwen touched his cheek lightly, aching to take his pain, to handle this for him. But she could not. He had to face this for himself. And it was better that he know. He was the only one who could take care of it. "Scott," she inquired gently, uncertainly, "you're ... not going to let them do that, are you? You're not going to let them destroy the evidence and sweep it under the rug? That's illegal, Scott."

He brought his eyes back to her with a great effort; still, he hardly seemed to be aware of her presence. "I don't know," he said somewhat hoarsely. "I don't think I—I wasn't prepared for this. You didn't know Ricky. You didn't know how ... I don't understand how ..." And he took a breath, shaking his head slowly. He closed his eyes again. "I don't think I can handle this. I don't think I want to."

Gwen wanted to enfold him in her arms, to hold him and comfort him, to do something to erase the past half hour from history, but she let her hand drop and she moved away from him. She went into the kitchen to retrieve her jacket and her purse, and then came back to the living room. She stood on the step leading to the foyer, looking at Scott sadly, helplessly. Her soul reached out to him. And she said quietly, firmly, "You're going to have to handle it, Scott. You have some heavy decisions to make. You're not the coal miner's son anymore. You're not Rick Stewart's little brother anymore—you're all grown up, and what has to be done now no one in the world but you can do."

His eyes met hers, hurt and dull and uncomprehending, and then Gwen felt the unexpected burn of tears rush to her throat. She quickly placed her hand on the doorknob, and she said softly, in a rush, "Call me when you need me." And she left him alone.

Chapter Twelve

Gwen waited two weeks. Twice during that period she tried to call Scott; on neither occasion did he answer his phone. She alternated between panic, despair, bitterness and, finally, resignation. Didn't he think she knew what he was going through? Didn't he know she wanted to share it with him, to help him? Didn't he know how much she cared?

But that was just it, of course. Scott did not know because she had never told him. She had never told him because there was a place deep inside her, yet unexplored, that refused to allow her to commit herself that deeply. And at the center of that secret place was fear.

At last a period of mourning set in. She had known from the beginning that it could not last, that they had built their tenuous relationship on hopes and passion, and its base was as transitory as sand. She had not expected it to end so quickly or hurt so much. The despair she felt when she was forced to face the fragility of what she had treasured so deeply and yearned for so strongly must have been much like what Scott had felt when he discovered the brother he had depended upon had never at all been what he seemed—just more illusions, shallow judgments, images that faded into nothing when held in close scrutiny.

She worried for Scott's safety, and she began to drive randomly by his house, just to check. His car was sometimes there, sometimes not, which meant at least he was moving around. He had not drunk himself into a stupor; he was not barricading himself alone with his grief; he had not succumbed to the depths of depression and done something rash. He was alive and functioning. He just did not want to see Gwen. How very, very little they had had if he could close her out so easily. She had known it all along.

Tim was worried about her, and so was Annalee. Gwen kept herself alert; she performed her duty with her usual brisk competency, and she had given no one cause for complaint. But the loss of her usual vitality was disturbing; she moved through her days mechanically, very much reserved, close to herself. Tim and Annalee questioned her, invited confidence, offered support. But Gwen only smiled a very false and brilliant smile and told them they were imagining things. She could not talk to either of them. Some things simply hurt too much to be shared.

She realized, after a time, that for a two-week-long relationship two weeks' mourning was more than enough. She knew that she had to sit down and examine it and put it into perspective, then forget about it. This was the point where she would evaluate all the facts, tell herself she would know better next time, and get on with her life.

Every night she promised herself she would do that...tomorrow.

Then one night as she sat in front of a flickering television screen, thinking about everything except the program, wrapped in a comfortable green terry robe, with her hair in fat, pink curlers, there was a knock on her door. Gwen's immediate reaction was suspicion, followed by alarm. Unexpected visitors at that hour were a rarity for Gwen, and this far from the highway it was unlikely that a stranded traveler would come to her door.

Gwen make her way to the door cautiously, flipped on the exterior light and made use of the peephole. She fumbled with the chain, flung open the door and then just stood there for what seemed like the longest time, staring at him. She should have been shocked; she should have been relieved, incredulous, angry, questioning, over-joyed—and perhaps she was, in fact, all of those things. But in the midst of those tumultuous emotions her hands flew to her roller-entwined hair and she snapped, "Well, what do you expect when you come banging on my door in the middle of the night? I don't look like a princess all the time, you know!"

Scott, whose face and eyes had been unreadable in the tricky light, began to smile. Then he began to chuckle. He placed his hands on her shoulders; he stepped forward and buried his face in her neck. "Ah, Wendy," he said softly, "I need a friend. Can I spend the night with you?"

There were kisses. There were arms holding each other, hands touching, eyes wondering—

tight, breathless embraces and low sounds of
hunger and joy. The past two weeks of agony and
uncertainty disappeared as though they had never
been. Scott was there; he was alive and well and
he had come back to her; the joy that filled her
was senseless and irrational, but that joy was all
that mattered. She just wanted to hold him and
touch him and never let him go.

Eventually they were inside. Eventually the first
frenzy passed, and they both knew there were
things that must be said. Gwen made coffee to
keep her hands busy, but she knew neither would
drink it. Her heart was pounding and her palms
were damp, and she knew that what he would say
to her in the next few minutes could send her
world crashing down around her feet again, or it
could build it bigger and stronger than ever. Why
had he come back? Why had he stayed away so
long? What decision had he made? Was this only
a formal good-bye, or had the weeks of separation
been only an interlude and was he now willing to
take up where they had left off?

Scott was sitting on the sofa when she returned,
the shadows of the television screen flickering on
his face. He looked so tired. He had aged in two
weeks. There were lines around his mouth that
had not been there before, and a new maturity in
his eyes. Gwen felt something small and essential
break in her heart for him.

But she smiled as she came toward him and
handed him his mug. "How about a cup of cream
and sugar?" she offered brightly.

He smiled as he accepted the mug, glanced at it
briefly, and then set it on the coffee table. Gwen

sat down and placed her cup beside his, waiting.

Scott slipped his arm around her shoulders. "I couldn't come here," he said simply, "until I worked this thing out for myself. Do you understand that, Wendy?" There was pleading in his eyes, and Gwen's own hurt was forgotten as she nodded.

"I wish you had let me help," she said softly.

Again, there was a fleeting hint of a smile, and he shook his head. "I couldn't have done this for myself if you hadn't already helped me, more than you know." He stroked her cheek with one knuckle, his eyes very quiet. "I'll always love you for that," he said.

Gwen swallowed hard. She did not want to hear any more words. She wanted to wrap her arms around him and draw him close; she wanted to reassure him and take reassurance from him in the most lasting, physical way. But she said, "What have you decided, Scott?"

He sighed. His hand dropped from her face and cupped her shoulder again. "It wasn't easy," he said. His voice was heavy as he reviewed the emotions of the past weeks. "At first I was so stunned—so disillusioned and hurt—that I didn't want to deal with it at all. God, I kept thinking, this is why Lyle never wanted me involved; I just wasn't strong enough or capable enough. And then I remembered what you said that day before you left." He smiled at her gently. "I'll bet you thought I didn't even hear you, didn't you? I remembered a lot you had said." And his voice fell slightly, taking him back to painful thoughts. "About growing up and being responsible...and

I knew that if Ricky hadn't left anything else of honor behind, he had left me. And I was the only one who could make decisions about what was going to affect my life.''

Again he released a breath; his hand tightened slightly on her shoulder, drawing her closer. Gwen rested her head on his arm, watching his face. It was a face that bore both the marks of suffering and the resolution of strength. He had endured his crucible and it had left scars, but as always, the act of survival gives more than it takes. Scott was not a different person now, just a better one. "Then, of course," he continued soberly, "once I had made that decision, the responsibility was almost overwhelming. How could I be sure that whatever I decided to do about the lawsuit wasn't motivated by anger or pride? There was a lot of anger," he said heavily. "I felt betrayed, dirtied, completely lost, and I just couldn't understand how I, who thought I knew him so well, could have been fooled. I couldn't understand why he had done it—I still don't, not completely." And his brow furrowed a little. "I guess I've never had to deal with that kind of pressure. When he was just getting started, when he needed that big break, when he had me and Ma in the background, waiting for him to rescue us, when the choice was between doing something a little bit wrong and starving..." A small, bitter smile touched the edge of his lips. "I keep remembering him saying to me, 'Whatever it takes, I'll come back for you.' And it makes a cold chill run down my spine. I don't know." There was a silence, and he lifted one shoulder helplessly. "Maybe all this

has something to do with why he was always doing good deeds, befriending the underdog, throwing away money by the fistful." He looked at
Gwen. "I still have a lot to work out in my head
about this," he told her simply. "I'd like to talk to
you about it sometime, maybe for a long time."

"We'll talk," she promised him softly, and her
hand caressed his neck. "Anytime you want, as
much as you want."

Scott smiled, with a quiet gratitude and a shared
understanding that transcended words. He caught
her hand, and kissed it briefly and held it as he
finished. "I still don't know if I've done the right
thing," he said quietly. "I spent some time with
Hampstead, and we talked—that helped." He
smiled, somewhat vaguely. "At least it helped
me, knowing what it felt like really to have the
responsibility of being in control. We're going to
settle out of court, but there won't be any denials
or any cover-ups, no more trying to buy people
out." A cloud came over his eyes. "Maybe I
should have fought harder to save Ricky's reputation. So many people are going to be disillusioned.
But then, maybe it's best that they know he
wasn't a god, just a real man who made real mistakes. Maybe the only good things that ever happen to people are when they have to face what's
real, what's behind all the illusions and makeup,
and deal with it." And he lifted one shoulder in a
helpless, resigned gesture. "I don't know. I just
know I've done the best I can with it. I hope it's
good enough."

There was a long silence. Gwen did not know
whether or not Scott was doing the right thing,

either, but he was not asking her approval. It was one of those decisions that had to be made between a man and his conscience, and outside judgments were irrelevant. But there was one thing she had to know. "And how do you feel," she asked softly, "about Rick Stewart now?"

He smiled at her, grateful for the question and the care that had prompted it. "A lot of things," he answered simply. "I don't think I'll really be entirely sure how I feel for a long time. But in a way..." He hesitated, choosing his words. "I know this is going to sound strange, but in a way I think I like him better with feet of clay. He cast a long shadow, and when I've adjusted a little better, I think I'm going to be happier not living in it. Besides—" and he smiled "—the legend was something he built; my brother was what he was. I guess I got so caught up in the image I forgot the man. Good and bad, just like the rest of us, not so perfect, capable of failing—he was my brother, and I'll always love him."

And in that moment all the pieces fitted together for Gwen. Over and over again she had asked herself who this man Scott Stewart was, what lay behind the constantly changing images and impressions she had formed of him. Now she knew. It was nothing simple, nothing clear, nothing that could be categorized. He was, like everyone else, a combination of everything that had made him: what he thought of himself, what others thought of him, what he was expected to be, what he wanted to be—good and bad, inconsistent and unpredictable, with traits that were admirable and traits that were simply individual. And in a crisis he was capable of drawing on inner strength and emerging victorious; he had found that inner part of himself that no one need understand but Scott, and he was capable of standing alone.

"I love you, Scott," Gwen said. It did not mean *I want you* or *I'm proud of you* or *I'm glad you're in my life*. It just meant that she loved him, all of him, for what he was.

The light that slowly built to a glow in his eyes was serene and everlasting, it warmed something deep in Gwen's soul. He reached forward slowly and began to remove the curlers from her hair, one by one, combing out the damp locks with his fingers. "Let's go to bed," he whispered.

THE NEXT DAY Gwen did something sinfully irresponsible. For the first time in her life, she called in sick. She unplugged the phone and spent the morning in bed with Scott. In the afternoon they walked on the beach; throughout the day they kept up a nonstop marathon of conversation. They talked about important things, like Rick Stewart, and unimportant things, like the best place to go for fillet of sole, but the communication in itself was a joy that was self-perpetuating. Just being together, talking to each other, touching each other, sharing those silent moments with their eyes and their smiles—those were the things that wove a bond between them that, at that time, it seemed nothing could break.

Then, unexpectedly, as Gwen was mixing cheeses for manicotti and Scott was stirring sauce, it happened.

"I want you to marry me," Scott said.

He said it so easily, so matter-of-factly, as though it were the most natural thing in the world. And, of course, it was. Gwen should have seen it coming a long time ago. But still, it started something cold trickling in her veins, something clammy curling in her stomach, and she could only stare at him.

Scott read it all in her expression. But still, all he allowed to cross his eyes was a momentary flicker of uncertainty, and the teasing smile he gave her seemed genuine. "I know, I know—not a very romantic proposal. I guess that's what they mean by popping the question. Give me another chance; I can do it better."

Gwen placed the bowl of cheeses on the counter and went to wipe her hands on a towel. Her heart was pounding dully. "Scott, I—"

"You're not going to give me any of that bull about it being too sudden or how we hardly know each other or how we only met a month ago." His tone was light, but genuine distress was darkening his eyes. Gwen had to look away from him.

"No." She drew the towel across her hands twice, three times; she made herself hang it back on the rack. She cleared her throat. "No, I just—"

"You said you loved me." There was no more teasing in his voice now. "I was hoping you meant the same thing by it that I did."

Distress tightened her face as she looked at him. "I did! I mean—I don't know!" She turned away quickly, fingertips playing over her throat nervously; she tried to think of something to say. "Scott, you've got to understand."

"All right," he replied equitably, "make me

understand." He leaned against the counter, his long, denim-encased legs crossed at the ankles, his weight on his elbows. His face was calm, his eyes shadowed. The sun caught chestnut sparks in his hair. So beautiful, so tender, he waited patiently—waiting for something she could not give him, expecting more than she had within her. An awful, burning knot formed in Gwen's throat, and she could not speak.

"I see," Scott said at last into the aching silence. With the passage of the moment, his face had grown hard, his eyes marble-smooth. A muscle that Gwen had never noticed before tightened along the edge of his jaw, and she could see the tightness of his shoulders and his neck. He was trying not to show his hurt and trying to keep the hurt from turning into anger. "So now we're not even talking." The words were short and cold. The edge of bitterness there cut Gwen.

She met his eyes bravely, and what she saw there almost made her flinch. It was an end of patience, an end of uncertainty, the last of her chances. "At least, before, you always had the decency to tell me to mind my own business when I started getting too close," Scott said, and the words came out with the pointed bite of a fistful of nails. The turbulence in his eyes was like a hostile sea, and she was the tiny vessel in imminent danger of being capsized by it. "Since the first moment I met you," he continued harshly, his hands bunching into restrained fists of anger and frustration, "you've given me everything except the one thing I wanted—you. I've never held back from you, have I?" he demanded. "Haven't I given

you the best of me? It may not have been much,
but it was all I had to give. I let you into my life, no
holds barred, nothing hidden—all I wanted from
you was a little of the same. But I guess that was
too much to ask. When I try to get you to talk
about yourself, you change the subject. When I
try to share your life, you draw some kind of curtain to keep me out. The only time you're completely with me is in bed, but I need more than
that, Wendy." The words had a terrible finality to
them, and his eyes were unrelenting. "We both
do."

Gwen turned away from him, holding her arms
at the elbows, aching inside. He was backing her
into a corner, making demands, asking promises.
She wanted to fight back, to lash out at him and
tell him to leave her alone, but already it was too
late for that, and she did not want him to leave her
alone. Why did he have to do this? Why couldn't
they just be the way they were? Why did he insist
upon more from her than she was willing to give?

Gwen knew what he wanted from her, but how
could she give it when she was not even sure it
existed? Certainty, permanence—how could she
give herself to a man when she was not certain
who she was?

"What we have between us is not going to go
away," Scott said. His voice was very quiet, but
tension and demand underlined every word. He
was angry. He had a right to be angry. "It doesn't
matter how long it's been there. It only matters
how deep it is. There is no place left for us to go
but into a commitment, Wendy. What frightens
you so much about that?"

She shook her head a little, and she cleared her throat again. "I'm not sure," she managed, still unable to look at him. "I'm not sure I'm capable of a commitment."

"Because of your mother?"

The statement was simple, flat, unsurprised, and a swift rush of gratitude and weakening affection rushed through Gwen. Of course he would understand. Of course Scott—tender, perceptive, sensitive—would know without words what Gwen had never confessed to anyone before. That she was afraid. That she did not know whether, when all the false images she had built about herself were torn down, there would be any stamina within her. That maybe, deep inside, she was really weak, like her mother . . . maybe she was a quitter, maybe she couldn't handle commitment, maybe the entire prospect would terrify her and she would run away, and that she was more frightened of hurting Scott than she was of hurting herself. But she could not put it into words. She simply nodded.

"You're not your mother, Wendy," Scott said roughly, "any more than I am my brother. You don't have to make the same mistakes she did."

Gwen knew that. She knew that there was a chance that, when all the layers were peeled away, Gwendolyn Blackshire would find exactly what she wanted to find in herself: A woman of strength, courage, judgment and certainty. A woman who always did the right thing. A woman who could be counted upon when things got rough. A woman who knew her purpose and never wavered from it. But the chances were equally as great that there would be nothing but a coward, a quitter, a person who folded under pressure. It was easy for Scott. He knew what he was made of. Could Gwen, in all conscience, offer him anything less?

"I don't like to make mistakes, Scott," she said simply. *Especially with a life as precious as yours.*

"Hell, who does!" His voice was a bark in the stillness of the kitchen. Gwen turned to him, startled, and his face was dark with impatience and frustration. "Do you think it was fun for me to find out what a big mistake I had made about Ricky? Don't you think I wished a thousand times I had just left it alone, never found out? Sure," he accused her, "the easiest way to avoid mistakes is never to get involved. Is that what you're going to do with the rest of you life, Wendy? Spend so much time trying to be perfect that you never let yourself be human?"

The tears that stung her lashes threatened to spill. She blinked them determinedly back. "I don't know, Scott," she answered unevenly.

She saw in the next moments a mixture of emotions cross his face—need, despair, stubbornness, anger, helplessness and, finally, hurt, the empty, aching hurt of loss and disappointment that nothing could ease. Beautiful Cupid, trusting and innocent, betrayed by the woman he loved while he slept—Gwen saw that bleakness of raw pain fill his eyes, and she knew that there was nothing she could say or do to make it better, nothing to ease the truth of her own uncertainty, nothing to bring him back to her.

"I expected more of you, Wendy," he said simply, quietly, and then he turned to go. But with his hand on the door handle, he turned back to her. The tenderness and the pain in his eyes were enough to break her heart. "Sometimes," he said quietly, "you just have to trust what you know deep down inside." And he opened the door. "If you ever find your answer, you know where to find me."

It wasn't until he was gone that Gwen bowed her head and cried.

Chapter Thirteen

Even through the fog of misery that surrounded her when she walked into the office the next morning, Gwen knew something was wrong. It was in the quick, sympathetic looks some of the officers gave her, in the way the others uncomfortably avoided her eyes. Even before she could question her, Annalee said, her face distraught, "Oh, Wendy, I tried to call you all day yesterday."

"What?" Gwen demanded, the tempo of her pulse speeding to immediate alertness. "What happened? What's wrong?"

Defeat crossed Annalee's face as she could find no way to soften the blow. "It's Tim," she said. "He's in the hospital. He was shot."

He had been shot while assisting state agents in a bust of the drug ring that had set up residence in an abandoned building off Highway 12 — a shoulder wound, serious but not critical. He would only be out of commission for a few weeks. All the while Gwen was driving to the hospital she kept thinking about it, replaying the imaginary scene in her head: Desperate situation, gunfire exchanged, officer down. She should have been there. Had she been performing her duty as she was supposed to—as she had done for the past two years of her life—she would have been in the middle of it, by Tim's side. She might have done something to make a difference. She might have been able to save him. Or she might have taken the bullet herself. The one time Gwen had behaved irresponsibly, the one time she had let down her guard and gone with her impulses, tragedy was the result. She should have been there.

The guilt was enormous, but beyond that, and even worse than that, was the nagging sense of relief. The drug bust was over. The thing she had feared the most had lived up to her worst nightmares, but it was over and she had not been involved. She did not have to dread every working day now. Her palms would not grow damp every time Mac handed out assignments. She would not come face-to-face with a crazed and desperate killer, wondering if she had the courage to pull the trigger. It was over. Destiny had slipped by her this time, and Gwen had nothing to fear.

Gwen was not very proud of herself as she walked into Tim's hospital room that morning.

"Hi ya, pardner." Tim grinned at her weakly as she opened the door, and Gwen thought bleakly, *Some partner.*

He did not look too bad. His color was poor and his eyes were dull, his bare chest and shoulder wrapped in bandages. But he was sitting up against the pillows, watching television, and he did not appear to be in too much pain.

Gwen swallowed hard and forced brightness into her tone as she came over to him. "Hi, yourself. What kind of con is this anyway, getting your-self shot just so you can take a few days off to watch soap operas and make passes at the nurses?''

He grinned and reached for her hand as she approached the bed. ''A pretty damn good one,'' he retorted, wrapping his fingers around hers.

Gwen looked at him, and all her willpower didn't seem to be able to keep those awful feelings of guilt and self-despair out of the way. She tried to smile, and she said a little uncertainly, ''I guess I should have brought you something—flowers, or candy, or ...''

He started to laugh, and winced. Something stabbed in Gwen's chest when she saw his pain. ''You can bring me the latest issue of *Hustler* next time you come,'' he told her.

And Gwen could not hide it any longer. ''Oh, Tim,'' she said miserably, sinking into the chair beside his bed. ''I feel just awful. I should have been there. If I had been there this might not have—''

He interrupted her with an impatient hiss. ''You know better than that. When it's your time, it's your time, that's all. Besides—'' he grinned ''—we got 'em.''

Gwen managed a weak smile. ''Yeah. You sure did.''

The silence that fell around them gradually became awkward, and Gwen could sense something about Tim change. He grew more serious, yet more reserved, a little uncertain. ''So,'' he said at last. His voice sounded strange. ''How's it going with your new boyfriend?''

Gwen sighed. The last thing Tim needed was to

be depressed by her problems. "Confusing," she said at last.

Tim tried to keep his tone light, but he couldn't hide his eyes, and they were serious. Very serious. "Well, if you can't get it worked out," he said, "there's always me."

Gwen stared at him, and she could not believe it. She started to make some light retort and caught it just in time. There was no mistaking it. Tim was trying to tell her something, something incredible.

And then he was no longer simply trying. "Ah, hell, Gwen," he said softly, and he glanced down at their entwined fingers. "You've probably already guessed. You've probably known for a long time. But yesterday, when I went down—well, you always think about things you wish you'd done and wish you'd done better, and one of the things that I wished I had done was to tell you—" he looked at her, not hoping, not pleading, just stating a fact "—that I've been in love with you for a long time."

Gwen's head reeled. She didn't know what to say. What could she say? This was Tim, whom she thought she knew inside out—they had been best friends since elementary school, their paths weaving in and out throughout adulthood—Tim, on whose sofa she had spent so many nights. She had never known. She had never had the slightest hint. How could she not have known? She was supposed to be so good at sizing people up, the expert at quick, efficient judgments—she knew nothing. *Nothing.*

"Tim, I—"

"Hey," he interrupted with a gentle laugh. "No need to look so panicky. It's not a problem. I realize—" And his eyes lowered briefly. "I figured out a long time ago that it's not in the cards for us. I probably just should've kept quiet about it. Only..." And now he looked at her, quietly, bravely. "I just thought you should know."

There was nothing Gwen could say. Nothing to apologize for, nothing to explain, and Tim knew that. He required nothing of her. But Gwen was shaken deeply. She might not be sure of herself; she might not be sure of Scott, but some things she had always been sure of. Now nothing made sense anymore.

She left the hospital in a daze. She felt as though she had failed Tim and herself. She should have been able to see what he felt for her. Not that there ever could have been anything between them—Tim knew that and so did she—but such genuine emotions should not have fallen on blind eyes. She should have known.

A long time ago—a lifetime ago; it seemed— Scott had told her, "Things are not always what they appear to be." Would she ever learn that lesson?

You're supposed to know these things, Wendy. You're supposed to be able to see the things that are going on around you. How can you be sure of your feelings about Scott when you can't even understand the things that are taking place right in front of your nose? She had make a mistake about Tim. How could she be sure of not making another quite different and far more drastic one with Scott?

Scott was waiting for a decision from her that

she could never make. She simply could not trust something as important as his happiness, as important as both of their entire lives, to her own frail powers of judgment.

Of course, the easiest way to avoid making mistakes is never to get involved.

Scott had a lot of faults, but that was not one of them. He had never been afraid of his own mistakes. He, who had far less confidence, experience and material wisdom than Gwen did, had never feared to commit himself, to get involved—with Gwen, about whom he knew nothing; with his brother's business, the end result of which had changed his life forever; with the truth. Gwen wished she had only half his courage.

Her mind was racing and tumbling as she got into her unit to resume patrol, filled with everything except concentration on her job. With only half her attention she heard Annalee's voice crackling on the radio, "Armed robbery in progress at Mason's Market, corner of Derring Street and Highway 12."

It might have been Gwen's distracted state of mind. It might have been residual guilt and confusion over Tim. It might have been some secret, desperate need to prove something to herself that caused Gwen to spin the unit around, to grab the microphone and return, "Unit Four in the vicinity. Responding." She knew it was wrong. She knew she should have waited for backup. She knew that allowing her judgment to be impaired by emotion was the biggest mistake an officer could make. But this time she did not stop to think; she simply acted.

IN RETROSPECT, it was like this: Gwen was out of
her unit, her weapon drawn, shielded by the open
door. Two suspects were fleeing the building.
One, young and lithe, with an automatic weapon,
veered away from her. The other, older, larger,
and with what appeared to be a sawed-off shotgun, was coming straight toward her and shouting. The entire episode, Gwen learned later, took
less than one minute. But a lot can happen in a
minute, and Gwen lived that one second by second.

She heard her voice shouting, "Police officer!
Drop your weapon!" and neither man responded.
She saw the wild-eyed man coming toward her,
waving the shotgun and shouting abuses. She saw
the fleet-footed one head for safety toward the
corner of the building. There was no time to stop
and think. It happened too fast to make a judgment. An officer was being threatened; procedure
was to shoot in self-defense.

She knew a thousand things in a single second.
She knew that if she shot the man coming toward
her at that range she would kill him. She knew if
she did not, he would kill her. She knew that it
made no sense for a criminal to run toward her
instead of away from her; she knew that it did not
have to make sense. She knew that if she did not
fire now she wouldn't get another chance. She
knew that she could not pull the trigger.

She felt all those things she had felt a hundred
times before; the cold palms, the frozen heart, the
paralyzed muscles, the raw and blinding terror.
She was the best shot on the force. She knew what
she was doing. She was enforcing the law. It was

up to her. *No choices, no decisions, just do what you have to do.*

But something was wrong. There was no time to think logically, no time to put the pieces together and form a picture. *Sometimes you just have to trust what you know deep down inside.* And Gwen knew deep down inside that something was wrong with this picture.

Where was the shopkeeper?

Scott's voice: *Things aren't always what they appear to be, Wendy.*

Annalee had not said whether there was more than one perpetrator. In a crime there were two elements, the criminal and the victim. How was she to know which one was which? And none of this was thought consciously; it was merely an intuitive knowledge quicker than a blinking eye, and her father's voice: *The only thing that's ever important to see clearly is what is inside yourself.*

Only seconds had passed. The man with the shotgun was almost upon her. The man who was running away was still within easy range.

This was it. Her moment of decision. And there was no time to make a decision.

You're solid gold, Wendy.

Trust what you know deep inside, Wendy.

Gwen raised her weapon. She fired.

Chapter Fourteen

Bits and pieces of the day played in the back of Gwen's mind like flashing still shots as she drove along the coastal highway toward home. Disassociated voices were the scraps of her recollection.

"Good thing you got here, Miss. I woulda shot the bastard myself, but my gun got jammed."

"Damn fool thing to do, Blackshire, going in alone. Why the hell didn't you wait for backup?"

"Pretty good shootin', Gwen."

"Hey, I only thought people shot the guns out of people's hands in the movies! How did you do that, anyway?"

"If that fool Mason had come at me with a sawed-off shotgun, I would've shot first and thought later. Doesn't he know it's against the law to keep a weapon like that in a private business?"

"How did you know he wasn't the bad guy?"

"Cool under pressure, that's our star officer."

"Good job, Deputy."

To all of this Gwen might or might not have replied. She might have told them that she had made a mistake in not waiting for backup and that she would never do anything so unprofessional again. She might have admitted that she had not intended to shoot for the hand, that the criminal had jerked around at the last moment and that it was only pure luck his injury had not been more serious. She might have said that she had recognized the shopkeeper at the last moment by the expression on his face or by the fear in his eyes or by the incoherent words he was shouting... or she might have confessed the truth and told them that she could not explain what had clicked within her in that split second that it mattered. It was just something she had known intuitively and without thinking, and she had acted upon it without reasoning.

Gwen might have told them that the last thing she was was cool under pressure. She might have confessed her terror, the fear of making a mistake, the lack of confidence in her own judgment that might have cost her her life that day. She might have told them that it was luck, pure and simple, and that the chances were equally as great that it could have gone the other way. But Gwen did not remember too much of what had happened after she pulled the trigger.

She knew that nothing of material consequence had occurred that day. She was an officer performing her duty, as she did every day of her life, as she would continue to do for as long as there was a place for her on the force. She deserved no special merit; she accepted no applause. But within Gwen something quiet and strong was beginning to blossom; she grew in the peace that can only come from having faced the worst and survived it.

Inside her peaceful little cottage nothing had changed. The sun splattered a benevolent silver over the lavender-and-blue living room, picking up the colors of changing waves, polishing a rich patina on wicker furniture. She smiled to herself as she crossed the room, touching things that meant familiarity and welcome to her. Her hand brushed across a small framed picture of her father, and she hesitated, picking it up. Her smile softened and then saddened as she looked at it.

"It took a long time," she said softly, touching the frame, "but I think I understand now. About Mother, about me—I hope you understand now, too." Gwen's father would have been proud of her today, but the cold reality Gwen finally had to face was how easily it could have gone the other way. There was nothing superhuman about Gwen, any more than there had been anything superhuman about her mother. Gwen had lived too much of her life blaming her mother for imagined failures, turning that blame into a fear of failure herself. Her mother had been nothing more than a woman, with weaknesses that weren't pleasant to look at, but weaknesses that must be acknowledged nonetheless. In a moment of crisis she had buckled. It could have happened to Gwen... but it hadn't. Today, it hadn't. But she knew her mother now; she understood her. And with that understanding came long-overdue forgiveness.

Gwen was aware of a sting of softening tears in her eyes as she replaced the photograph, but they weren't tears of sadness. Just resignation.

She left the room and turned on the taps for a

shower, and, within her, tumultuous emotions and random thoughts were beginning to settle into an orderly pattern. Scott had said that some of the best things that happened to people happened when they were forced to see the truth that lay behind the illusions and had to deal with it. Gwen, convinced she was wiser, more competent and more in control than Scott, had not really paid much attention to him. Scott had learned sooner the same lesson she had had to face only today, and it was something each of them had to go through on their own. They could share the understanding now, if Scott would have her.

Did Scott still want her?

Gwen knew this wasn't the end. A crisis had been met and passed, but that did not mean it wouldn't come again. Maybe she would still be scared. Maybe next time her judgment would be wrong. One day she would make a mistake. But this time she had been right. This time she had taken a chance when all the odds were against her, and she had won. Today she had done battle with her demon and found it not so invincible as she had imagined. She had found that place deep inside her that was the final truth about Gwen Blackshire: The place of weaknesses and strengths, of good and bad, of rights and wrongs; a woman who sometimes made mistakes; a woman who could take chances when she had to; a woman whose judgments were sometimes shallow and misguided, but sometimes correct; a woman capable of making the right decision when it counted. No, this was not the end of self-discovery and adjustment, but only the beginning. She had a long way to go, but she could trust herself to deal with whatever lay ahead. And she was no longer afraid of the journey.

Gwen changed into jeans and a sweater, then brushed her hair absently, not even seeing her reflection in the mirror. She wanted to tell Scott. She wanted to be with him. He had gone through an awful pain of discovery, and she had tried to sympathize, to be supportive; she had done the best she could, but in the end she had failed him because she could not give him the one thing he had asked from her. She had not been able to understand fully even what he wanted until she had traveled that same lonely road by herself. She could come to him now a wiser person, a stronger person . . . if he still wanted her.

If you ever find the answer, he had said, *you know where to find me.*

The reflection in Gwen's mirror tightened slowly with lines of resolve; she placed the hairbrush on the dresser and scooped up her keys. She did not think about it any more. All he had asked from her was all she had to offer him: Herself, not perfect, not infallible, not invincible—just a woman who was willing to try, for the man she loved, to be the best she could be.

GWEN PARKED THE CAR in front of the house on Beachwood Lane and started up the wide driveway. She smiled to herself when she recalled how this place had looked to her one night barely a month ago. She would never have guessed then that one day it would look like home to her—

which only goes to show how little can be learned from first impressions.

She climbed the steps; she lifted her hand to the door, behind which someone was waiting to hear her answer. Scott opened it before she even knocked.

His expression was at first surprised, then welcoming, then quickly confused and a little wary. His eyes filled with questions. He opened his mouth to speak, but Gwen did not give him a chance.

"You told me," she said, "when I found my answer, to let you know."

His eyes searched hers quickly, hesitantly, seeing it there already but almost afraid to believe. His voice was a little hoarse. "And . . . have you?"

She nodded firmly, and the happiness of certainty flooded her as she saw the welcome in his eyes. "It's yes," she said, and stepped into his arms. He held her. He wrapped his arms tightly around her, burying his face in her hair with a deep breath of unquestioning joy and gratitude. She pressed her cheek against his shoulder; she felt his heart beat against hers, and she relaxed against him in utter contentment. "Yes, Scott," she whispered. "To everything."

H·A·R·L·E·Q·U·I·N

FIRST·CLASS
Sweepstakes

OFFICIAL RULES

1. NO PURCHASE NECESSARY. To enter, complete the official entry/order form. Be sure to indicate whether or not you wish to take advantage of our subscription offer.

2. Entry blanks have been preselected for the prizes offered. Your response will be checked to see if you are a winner. In the event that these preselected responses are not claimed, a random drawing will be held from all entries received to award not less than $150,000 in prizes. This is in addition to any free, surprise or mystery gifts which might be offered. Versions of this sweepstakes with different prizes will appear in Preview Service Mailings by Harlequin Books and their affiliates. Winners selected will receive the prize offered in their sweepstakes brochure.

3. This promotion is being conducted under the supervision of Marden-Kane, an independent judging organization. By entering the sweepstakes, each entrant accepts and agrees to be bound by these rules and the decisions of the judges, which shall be final and binding. Odds of winning in the random drawing are dependent upon the total number of entries received. Taxes, if any, are the sole responsibility of the prize winners. Prizes are nontransferable. All entries must be received by August 31, 1986.

4. The following prizes will be awarded:

   (1) Grand Prize: Rolls-Royce™ *or* $100,000 Cash!
   (Rolls-Royce being offered by permission of
   Rolls-Royce Motors Inc.)

   (1) Second Prize: A trip for two to Paris for 7 days/6 nights. Trip includes air transportation on the Concorde, hotel accommodations...PLUS...$5,000 spending money!

   (1) Third Prize: A luxurious Mink Coat!

5. This offer is open to residents of the U.S. and Canada, 18 years or older, except employees of Harlequin Books, its affiliates, subsidiaries, Marden-Kane and all other agencies and persons connected with conducting this sweepstakes. All Federal, State and local laws apply. Void in the province of Quebec and wherever prohibited or restricted by law. Winners will be notified by mail and may be required to execute an affidavit of eligibility and release, which must be returned within 14 days after notification. Canadian winners will be required to answer a skill-testing question. Winners consent to the use of their name, photograph and/or likeness for advertising and publicity purposes in conjunction with this and similar promotions without additional compensation. One prize per family or household.

6. For a list of our most current prize winners, send a stamped, self-addressed envelope to: WINNERS LIST, c/o Marden-Kane, P.O. Box 10404, Long Island City, New York 11101

SWRL·A·1

Discover the new and unique

Harlequin Gothic and Regency Romance Specials!

Gothic Romance	Regency Romance
DOUBLE MASQUERADE	TO CATCH AN EARL
Dulcie Hollyock	Rosina Pyatt
LEGACY OF RAVEN'S RISE	TRAITOR'S HEIR
Helen B. Hicks	Jasmine Cresswell
THE FOURTH LETTER	MAN ABOUT TOWN
Alison Quinn	Toni Marsh Bruyere

A new and exciting world of romance reading

Harlequin Gothic and Regency Romance Specials!

Available in September wherever paperback books are sold, or through Harlequin Reader Service:

Harlequin Reader Service
In the U.S.
P.O. Box 52040
Phoenix, AZ 85072-9988

In Canada
P.O. Box 2800, Postal Station A
5170 Yonge Street
Willowdale, Ontario M2N 6J3

CR-C-1

You're invited to accept 4 books and a surprise gift Free!

Acceptance Card

Mail to: **Harlequin Reader Service**®

In the U.S.
2504 West Southern Ave.
Tempe, AZ 85282

In Canada
P.O. Box 2800, Postal Station A
5170 Yonge Street
Willowdale, Ontario M2N 6J3

YES! Please send me 4 free Harlequin American Romance® novels and my free surprise gift. Then send me 4 brand new novels as they come off the presses. Bill me at the low price of $2.25 each —an 11% saving off the retail price. There are no shipping, handling or other hidden costs. There is no minimum number of books I must purchase. I can always return a shipment and cancel at any time. Even if I never buy another book from Harlequin, the 4 free novels and the surprise gift are mine to keep forever.

154 BPA-BPGE

Name	(PLEASE PRINT)	
Address		Apt. No.
City	State/Prov.	Zip/Postal Code

This offer is limited to one order per household and not valid to present subscribers. Price is subject to change.

ACAR-SUB-1

Readers rave about
Harlequin American Romance!

"The stories are great from beginning to end."

    —M.W., Tampa, Florida

"...excellent new series...I am greatly impressed."

    —M.B., El Dorado, Arkansas

"I am delighted with them...can't put them down."

    —P.D.V., Mattituck, New York

"Thank you for the excitement, love and adventure your books add to my life. They are definitely the best on the market."

    —J.W., Campbellsville, Kentucky

*Names available on request.